I0746017

The Box

A Carrie Border Novella

Nancy Jackson

WILD IDEAS PRESS

Paperback - 978-1-7348946-7-7
eBook - 978-1-7348946-6-0

Published in the United States by Wild Ideas Press LLC
Yukon, Oklahoma

Book Cover Design by
Angela Westerman of
AK Organic Abstracts
AKOrganicAbstracts.com

Each time I write a novel there are so many people I would like to dedicate it to. I have dedicated past novels to my wonderful children, Ben, Lacey, and Kendon, and their children, my amazing grandchildren. I've dedicated them to my Father God. Nothing I create is done outside of him.

It has been four years since I've completed a novel. As I sit here my mind is drawn to my dear friend, Vicki Thorp. She has been a constant friend both encouraging and laughing with me along the way. So, today I dedicate this novel to her. Thank you Vicki. You are a true gem!

Contents

Chapter One

She was old enough to know that panic caused a person to use more oxygen than normal. She was also old enough to know that the small enclosed space she was in was just about out of that precious commodity.

When she first woke, she did panic. The confines were so tight that she could barely move. Her legs could not shift into any other position other than straight out. She could not bend her elbows. When she tried to lift her head, it quickly bounced off of the ceiling of the enclosure.

No light at all trickled in and the sound was deadly nonexistent. Time was a fictitious entity that had no place in this space. It neither stood still nor sped up. There was no escape.

She forced herself to calm down into a place where she consumed as little oxygen as possible. That was her focus as tears slipped down the sides of her face and puddled in her ears.

Chapter Two

The sun shot Carrie right in the eye as she turned to look out the window. She squinted and turned back towards her desk.

"What is the date today?" she asked Randy instead of looking at her calendar.

He didn't answer, only looked at her. When she met his gaze, she laughed. "Well, what is the date?"

He shook his head, his dark thick hair shifting and falling onto his forehead. "It is, my lazy co-worker, Tuesday June 20, 2012. Why?"

She smiled knowingly, "Today is your anniversary. Did you forget?"

The color drained from his face, and his eyes shifted back and forth in panic. He then looked straight at Carrie, "Oh crap!"

Carrie belly laughed and began wiping tears away while Randy was desperately searching for a florist who could deliver on such short notice. *He and Sandy have only been married for two years. How could he forget?*

Randy busied himself as Carrie watched the room. The floor where their desks were stationed held ten other agents with the state investigative unit for the state of Oklahoma. What had just been a calm and easy atmosphere in the room had quickly shifted. Carrie took notice and walked over to a small group of agents.

"What happened?" she asked.

Agent Dirk James turned to her. "We've had an alert. A thirteen-year-old girl has gone missing. Her parents reported her missing to the Oklahoma City Police Department a week ago. Their leads have dried up and they've asked us to join the investigation."

"What can I do?" asked Carrie.

"Grab your partner and meet us in the conference room."

In less than five minutes, the room was filled with all available agents and their Special Agent in Charge John Bracket. Nervous tension filled the room and several of them shifted from foot to foot, eager to begin.

"Ok, let's get quiet," said Bracket. We have a thirteen-year-old girl last seen in Warr Acres around MacArthur and 63rd Street. She had walked to the Walgreens on the corner. While there, she purchased a Dr. Pepper and a bag of Gardettos. No one in the store saw which direction she went when leaving the store, but she should have gone back to the east, towards her home. She lived only about a quarter mile from the store.

"It was 4:30 in the afternoon of last Tuesday. Her parents didn't arrive home from work until around 5:30 and 5:40 individually. She was not there when they arrived. There was a note from her that she had gone to Walgreens, but nothing about what time she had gone there. They waited for about ten minutes, then the father drove towards Walgreens, taking the route he knew she usually took. He spoke with the clerk at the store who told her that he had seen her but she had left.

"They then proceeded to call the OKCPD, who pulled video footage from Walgreens. She did indeed head east towards her home. There were no other businesses or residences between Walgreens and her home with exterior video cameras." Bracket laid the pages he was reading from on the podium and pulled off his reading glasses. He closed his eyes, and pinched the bridge of his nose.

"What about her phone? I assume that is being tracked," said Agent James Finch.

Bracket was already shaking his head before James finished. "She didn't have a phone. Her parents were restrictive in that manner and weren't going to buy her a phone until she was sixteen."

Bracket picked the papers back up. "Her name is Melinda Banner, thirteen years old. Long dark hair, green eyes, and about 105 pounds. She is five feet two inches tall. Here is a sheet with the details."

The room came to life again as the agents passed around a short stack of papers containing her picture and pertinent details. Carrie looked at the young girl's face. Her teeth were slightly crooked, and she had freckles that scattered delicately across her nose. Carrie loved her immediately, then chided herself for it.

A sharp jab in her side startled Carrie, and she realized Bracket had just addressed her and Randy and was waiting for a response.

"We're on it, chief," Randy said.

Carrie nodded and turned towards the conference room door as she walked back towards her desk. She was still rebuking herself for opening up emotionally when looking at the girl. But she was such a darling that she had captured Carrie's heart before she even realized it.

Melinda didn't know how long she had been confined before she woke up in the box, or how long it had been since she had woken up. She was getting sleepy though, and that meant she would soon fall asleep and never wake up again.

It felt to her as though she were in a metal box. She didn't know enough about metal to even guess, whether it was steel, aluminum, or something else.

Her ears strained to hear any noise at all, but it was oppressively quiet. She sensed, though, that the box was underground, which terrified her. There was a slight smell that she associated with helping her mother in their backyard garden. Dirt. She was buried in a metal box in the dirt. She willed herself not to panic at that revelation.

The box was so narrow that arms were pinned to her sides. She could, however, slightly bend her elbows up to press her palms against the ceiling of the box. She tried pushing, but the angle of her arms didn't allow her to put any weight or force behind the movement.

Determined to do what she could, she persisted in trying to angle her arms to gain more traction to push on the lid, to no avail. It wasn't long until her energy was spent and she dropped her hands back down to her sides in resignation.

Working to get out was expending precious air, but what choice did she have? And how would she know what was the right choice? Work to get out, or wait?

She hadn't ever gone to church, but she had a friend who talked about praying sometimes and wondered if that would work for her. She didn't know how to pray, so she only said, "Please God, help me. I don't know how to pray, but I need you to rescue me, please."

There was no hope for her to grasp onto though, and she broke down completely. Her small body wracked with sobs, convulsing against the walls which reinforced the limits of her narrow captivity.

Her crying slowed, and then she drifted away.

Chapter Three

"Who are the detectives assigned to the case?" Carrie asked.

"It looks like Matthew Booker, or Matt, is the lead. Not sure who else will work with him on this one," Randy replied as he shuffled papers on his desk. While Carrie stood waiting for him to give her a directive, he picked up the phone and dialed.

"Hey Matt, this is Randy Jefferies at the OSBI."

Carrie listened as they briefly discussed meeting to go over the case file, which resulted in Randy confirming that Matt would be right over.

"What can we do in the meantime?" Carrie was anxious to get started. She knew that time was not on their side and even though they were approaching it as a search and rescue, she feared that in truth, it would turn out to be a body recovery.

Since the tragic loss of her parents, she had built solid walls around her emotions to ward off any future pain from loss. She had succeeded in pushing her fiancé away, and she was still stacking bricks both deep and wide on her emotional wall.

But when she had seen that girl's sweet face, her heart had crumbled. Carrie shook her head at the memory and became determined to get even more stalwart in her emotional shutdown. At that resolve, she felt herself harden just a little bit more.

The smell of cinnamon rolls suddenly distracted Carrie from her internal shutdown. She looked up and saw Sherri Valencia walking into the middle of the room. She carried two large boxes of Aunt Annie's cinnamon rolls.

Carrie watched Sherri's endearing smile fade as Agent James Finch intercepted her visit. Sherri nodded as they spoke, then laid a hand on James' shoulder and slightly dipped her head, closing her eyes.

Sherri was the designated chaplain for the OSBI. It wasn't a permanent or even a paid position, but one that many agents believed was essential.

Carrie liked Sherri, but was confused and bewildered by the way seasoned agents allowed themselves to be drawn to a non-logical place to do their job. Carrie could not reconcile how bowing one's head and mumbling some words could possibly help find this girl, or any other girl, for that matter.

James beamed at Sherri and patted her arm. As he walked away, she turned towards Carrie. The agitation that Carrie felt was irrational, she knew, but she felt herself pulling her arms tighter around herself, all the same.

Sensitive compassion rested on Sherri's face. Carrie knew it was genuine, but she remained guarded against its disarming qualities.

"How are you Carrie?"

Carrie plastered on one of her best fake smiles, "I'm good. Busy with this recent case, though." She hoped Sherri would take the hint and leave. *Why on earth does being around Sherri make me so nervous?*

Sherri watched Carrie with what seemed like an uncanny

knack for sensing beyond the surface. Carrie could feel herself begin to fidget, and quickly dropped her hands. "You brought cinnamon rolls from Aunt Annie's?"

"Yes, would you like one?"

"Soon. I'd love one here in a little bit." Carrie nodded nervously and wrapped her arms back around her middle.

"Okay." Sherri gave a quick nod and turned to leave. Then, almost as an afterthought, she looked back at Carrie. "The girl will be okay, Carrie."

Carrie was speechless. How could she possibly know such a thing?

"Yeah, okay. Thanks," was all Carrie could respond with.

Suddenly, Randy re-appeared and began herding Carrie towards an empty workroom. "Here." He shoved a rolling white-board towards her as he grabbed several erasable markers. They used the room for group collaboration on cases. There was a long work table and several metal chairs.

Randy used a red marker to write Melinda's name and details from the flyer at the top of the board. Carrie hoped they would soon fill it with leads and suspects.

The agents heard Detective Booker long before he reached the room. His booming voice echoed down the hall and into the room.

"Hey there. I see I found you."

He walked into the room with a small box of case files. The box was so empty that the few files it contained wouldn't even stand upright.

Introductions were made, and Carrie immediately began pulling out the files. "There is hardly any information in here." She expressed her frustration as she turned the pages.

"I know. We have no leads and as it often is, no one saw anything." Matt sounded equally frustrated, and Carrie was empathetic.

Carrie looked up at him. "Where do we start?"

"The patrol officers have combed every inch of the normal path and alternate paths she might have taken. They collected anything that might even possibly be hers. We had her parents look through all of it, but nothing surfaced as being hers.

"Detective Rick Morris and I sat with the parents and gathered the names and contact info of all of her friends. At least the known friends."

"Why do you say that?" Carrie asked.

"Because most teenagers have at least a few friends their parents are not aware of."

Carrie nodded, deep in thought, thinking back to her own youth. She had felt so free with her parents that she was never hesitant to share her friends with them. But, she supposed, there may have been a few that she never brought home or talked about.

"Rick and I have made it through the entire list of friends. No one heard from her on that day and they had nobody else to add to the list.

"And now you have hit a wall, hoping we might think of something you haven't," said Randy with a slight smile.

Matt shrugged and turned up his hands. "It's a dead end unless you guys turn something up."

The reality hit Randy hard, and he nodded. "Thanks. We will see what we can do."

~

A hand was shaking Melinda. It rested on her upper chest and was gently shaking back and forth.

She felt groggy, and the sun was now shining full force down on her. Confusion filled her mind as she slowly came back to reality. When she did, she jerked back from the source of the hand and began pushing it away.

"Hey. Hey now. I'm here to help you." It was the voice of an older woman, but Melinda couldn't see her face clearly. The sun was a powerful back-light and she could only see a silhouette. "Who are you? Why am I here?"

"I'm Peggy. Peggy Bishop. I don't know why you are here. I was just out for a walk and came across this metal box and thought I would look and see what was in it. And there you were."

Melinda rose slowly to a sitting position, looking around to see where she was.

"Let me help you out of there." Peggy stepped back in an effort to alleviate the girl's anxiety. She reached down, offering a hand.

Melinda took the hand and allowed Peggy to help her out of the box. It looked to be aluminum, and the top was flush with the ground. It had a hinged lid with a lip that slid down over the sides of the box about two inches. There was a latch opposite of the hinged side that someone could lock or just latch shut.

As Melinda looked around, she realized they were on the edge of a deeply wooded area near a small creek.

"Where are we?" Melinda's face shifted from fear to anger.

"Not far from my house. I was out walking when I saw the box. Good thing I did, or you would still be trapped." Peggy had a soft and calming demeanor.

Suddenly, gratitude for her rescue broke Melinda free from her fear and she lunged toward Peggy in a full-body bear hug. "Thank you so much! I thought I was going to die in there." Tears were streaming down her dirt covered face.

Peggy received the embrace and held Melinda in a gentle and loving hug. But what Melinda couldn't see was the look of satisfaction on Peggy's face. It had worked. Her captive was now grateful to her savior. Just the way Peggy wanted it.

Chapter Four

It was a beautiful day. It wasn't too hot, and the wind was barely a breeze, which was incredibly abnormal for Oklahoma. But Carrie hardly felt the beauty surrounding her. She couldn't shake the sadness that had settled inside of her heart like a dead weight. No matter what they had tried, they still had no leads.

They had been out interviewing the leads in the files, and were just leaving the Walgreen's where Melinda was last seen. They knew the OKCPD would do a good job with initial contact, but the agents felt it was vital for them to connect with everyone they could. It grounded them to the case and gave them a sense of where they were and what they needed to do.

"What now?" Carrie asked as Randy walked up. The absence of hope on his face mirrored her own.

Randy stopped and stood looking off. He crimped his brow, deep in thought. He tilted his water bottle up and swigged heartily.

As he twisted the cap back on, he looked at Carrie, still frowning.

"Nothing more we can do for now. I hate thinking we've exhausted all leads, but there is no one we haven't talked to and nowhere we haven't looked." He seemed to search Carrie's face expectantly, hoping she might come up with something he hadn't thought of. She had one of the most brilliant investigative minds he had ever known.

But Carrie just shook her head. They both walked back to their SUV with heavy hearts and laden feet. Both were individually searching the deep recesses of their minds for anything that had not occurred to them, but nothing came.

"I hate admitting that a case has grown cold on my watch," said Randy as Carrie climbed in to sit beside him.

He shifted into gear and pulled out into the traffic.

"Can you take me home? I need to call my parents. They can come get me." Melinda rattled on with the excitement of being out of the box, but her joy would soon be diminished.

"Where do you live?" asked Peggy

As Melinda rattled off her address, the look on Peggy's face caused Melinda to slow and then stop. "What?" Melinda asked.

"That is a very long way from here. I don't have reliable transportation either."

Melinda's mouth hung open in shock. "What do you mean? Where are we?"

Lies rolled off Peggy's tongue as easily as the truth did for most people. "We are in Nebraska on my parents' farm. They left it to me when they passed. We are about sixty miles from the nearest town."

How could we be so far from my home? Melinda wondered. "That's fine. Just get me to your phone. I am sure my parents will come and get me."

"No can do. I've never had a phone. Don't like 'em. Don't want 'em," Peggy lied.

"So how am I going to get home?" Melinda's incredulous tone didn't seem to faze Peggy. "I do appreciate you rescuing me. But I need to contact my parents. They have to be worried sick." Melinda looked up into Peggy's face and studied it. She looked like such a nice older lady and after all, she had rescued Melinda.

"We will think of something," Peggy smiled assuredly back at the girl's charming face. "Yes, we'll think of something. But in the meantime, you can stay with me." Peggy put her hand gently on Melinda's back and ushered her away from the silver box.

Something in the air had shifted and the hair on the back of Melinda's neck stood up as a subtle warning. The trust she initially had for Peggy was rapidly waining.

What if this Peggy was not what she seemed and wouldn't let her leave? It was then that she realized she was already planning her escape.

As soon as they walked back into their office, Carrie and Randy were met with another flyer from Agent Finch. "Matt Booker just sent this over. Another young teenage girl has turned up missing. Same thing as Melinda. She was only a couple of blocks from her home. The parents have been questioned and neighborhood video scanned. Nothing."

Carrie's posture crumpled. "Melinda's case has been one dead end after another, and now this one? Are you sure it's connected? I know there are similarities in ages, but there could be different reasons for the disappearances."

Randy looked at the face of Emily Smith, age twelve. She had sandy blonde hair and blue eyes. She seemed small for her age, with a pixie-like physique.

"Okay," Randy said. "We'll talk to Matt and see what he knows."

Carrie's stomach clenched. She had started with the OSBI only two years prior. She wasn't a newbie, but she still didn't feel fully confident in her role as investigator. Yes, her degrees in criminology and forensic science had supplied her with valuable information. But she had learned there were some things that only experience could teach you.

So much of it was developing an instinct for the psychology of criminals. How they operated and why they did what they did. That aspect was always somewhat changing, so law enforcement was often caught off guard when someone veered from the expected trajectory. However, there were still a lot of consistencies across the board in the whats and the whys.

Taking young girls could mean many things. It could be the horror of a psychopath just needing to kill, with a fetish for teens. Girls could be taken to be sold as captives in a human trafficking ring. There wouldn't be a body to find, and the success of finding them at all was low.

There were always those sick bastards who preferred young teen girls for sexual pleasure, raping and then killing them. Carrie still, after so many years in law enforcement with the OKCPD and now with the OSBI, couldn't wrap her mind around that. And she refused to let her heart go there.

Randy's voice stirred her out of her deep thoughts. "Matt is headed over to the Lakeview Diner for lunch. He suggested we meet him there."

"Okay," Carrie said and fell into step behind him as he headed for the door.

"This never gets easier," said Randy glancing over at Carrie. He knew she was struggling with this case. She was very good, but the kinds of cases that involved children were difficult to bear.

"It has to get easier, doesn't it? Otherwise, how do you cope with it?"

"No, it doesn't get easier, but you learn a little more with each case on how to cope. How to disassociate from it a bit. You just have to, or it will prevent you from seeing the case clearly. You learn to step back and see all aspects clearly. Dwelling on the emotion of it will fog your thoughts."

Carrie had learned to wall off her emotions to a degree in her personal life, but not in this respect. She resolved once again to do better, become even harder.

Once at the diner, Carrie saw it was still a bit early for the business lunch crowd, so parking was plentiful. Matt was in a booth with a good vantage point of the inside and outside of the restaurant. Next to him sat another detective that Carrie knew from an earlier case, Rick Morris.

Carrie nodded in acknowledgment and slid into the booth next to Rick. The smell of burgers, fries, and pie melded into an intoxicating elixir that reminded Carrie of her hunger.

"We haven't ordered yet," said Matt. "We just got here."

A waitress saw Randy and Carrie arrive and hurried over with menus. She took their drink orders, and Carrie stared at the menu in her hands. She was hungry, and her stomach attested to it, but the thought of eating while two young girls were possibly going without made it hard for Carrie to enjoy food.

Finally, she made her decision. She snapped the menu shut and laid it on the table.

Chapter Five

It was a long walk back to Peggy's house. The sun was bearing down and dust stuck to the sweat on Melinda's body. The bugs were constantly assaulting her as well. She spent most of the walk shielding her eyes from the sun and swatting bugs. She was miserable, thirsty, and ready to be home, but thankful to be out of the box.

Finally, she noticed they were approaching a worn down little farmhouse. The white paint was peeling a little and the yard would never win any prizes.

Melinda looked around. There were no other houses apparent anywhere, and the driveway was so long that she couldn't see the end. There was no paving, only rough ruts from being driven on when muddy. Few would drive a nice car over that.

A chicken caught Melinda's attention, and she jumped. She had never been around them and didn't know how to respond. *Will they bite me?*

"Don't mind those chickens. They are just curious who my new friend is. They won't hurt you," Peggy said as she pulled the squeaky back door screen open.

Melinda hesitated before walking up the two crooked concrete steps to what appeared to be the back door. Thirst, and a need to get out of the heat, spurred her through the door. At first glance, it appeared Peggy kept a tidy home. There were no dishes in the sink, or anything out of place on the Formica countertop. The kitchen linoleum, though cracked and faded, looked clean at least.

"Can I have some water?" Melinda asked with hesitation.

"Of course you can." Peggy retrieved a glass from the cabinet and filled it with clear tap water. She handed it to Melinda with a smile. "Don't drink it too fast now."

It was hard to resist. The water tasted good and was cool straight from the well. After a large drink or two, Melinda forced herself to slow down. "Thank you. I was so thirsty. I don't know how long I was in there. I thought I was going to run out of air."

Concern showed on Peggy's face. "Thankfully, I don't think the seal on that lid was tight enough to keep out all of the air."

"But it was totally dark."

"Probably from the lip over the edge. There was a bit of dirt shoved over the edge, too. But I knew when I saw that big silver patch that something wasn't right. It was easy to swipe the dirt off and find the clasp.

"Would you like a shower now? You look so hot and dirty. I can wash your clothes."

Melinda craved the cool water of a shower rushing over her and nodded. "These are all the clothes I have," she said, looking down and pulled at her sweaty top.

Peggy looked at Melinda, assessing her size. "Well, I think I might have something you can wear while yours dry."

The bathroom matched the rest of the old farmhouse. A claw-foot bathtub with a shower overhead and a shower curtain that had seen better days. The linoleum matched that in the kitchen and the old mirrored cabinet over the sink had dark patches where the mirror backing had worn away. But again, Melinda observed, it was clean.

There was also a small window beside the tub and Melinda noticed it was made so that you could raise and lower the bottom half. She stored that observation away in her mind as a possible exit.

"Here you go." Peggy hustled into the room with a small stack of clothing. "You are a lot smaller than I am, but my niece left these things here when she stayed with me a while back. I think you two are pretty close in size." She handed the stack to Melinda, who was standing aimlessly in the middle of the bathroom.

Peggy reached down and turned on the tub faucet, checking the water temperature periodically to make sure it was acceptable. When done, she opened a cupboard door and pulled out a clean, fluffy towel and washcloth.

"Here you go. There is soap and shampoo right there," she pointed to the edge of the tub. Peggy smiled what she hoped was a reassuring smile and left the room, pulling the door closed behind her.

Melinda stayed in the shower, washing and enjoying the flush of the water as it cleansed her skin. The pulsing water also released the tension of the past few days and she felt herself begin to relax.

She could not understand how she had wound up in the box. Her memory was distorted and faded. She had lost a large portion of her memory which included how she had come to be in the box. Those thoughts gripped her stomach in fear. But she was safe now, and she forced herself to calm down.

Finally, as the water grew cooler, she shut it off and climbed out. The towel she wrapped herself in was fluffy and felt good against her skin. The small window once again caught her eye. Peggy seemed sympathetic enough and Melinda felt they could work out a solution together to help get her back home, but just in case...

Melinda dropped the towel and reached for the window. It wouldn't budge. Years of paint had sealed it completely shut. Disappointment unexpectedly engulfed Melinda.

The day had felt extremely long to Carrie. She needed some kind of distraction to get her mind and her heart off of the missing girls.

She pulled into the bar that was only about a mile from her house. She had made the rounds at too many of the bars in the area, and realized that staying close to home was a better idea. Less of a chance for getting a DUI. Of course, she knew better than to drink and drive. That is why she made it a point to not be too far away. If she had to, she could get a taxi home and then walk back in the morning to get her car.

This had been her hangout for the past eight months and the regulars had since welcomed her into their group. The ones who, like her, didn't want to go straight home from work without a drink or two in them first.

Carrie didn't want to go home any more except to sleep. That was her way of coping. Coping with the loss of her parents two years ago and losing Billy, her fiancé. She knew losing Billy was her own fault. She had pushed him away, angry at the world, and couldn't bring herself to even attempt to undo what she had done.

It was those realities that kept her drinking after work. Avoidance. That was her closest friend.

The group waved her over to the pool table at the back of the room. Only three tonight. The truck driver Benny, about fifty-five, she guessed. And then there was Simon, a welder, and Boots, who was currently between jobs. Those last two were around her age, late twenties or early thirties. She couldn't tell and didn't care.

Wade, the bartender, brought her usual mug of draught beer, and set it on the tall table Carrie was leaning on.

"Thanks Wade," Carrie flashed a quick smile towards the forty-something bartender as she lifted the mug. She closed her eyes, tilted her head back slightly and let the foamy elixir slowly coast down her throat. She didn't stop until half of the mug was in her stomach.

She used her arm to swipe some foam off of her mouth as she savored the warmth that the beer was sending out from inside her. Just before she tilted the mug up for one more deep swig, she motioned to Wade for another.

"Hard day?" asked Simon.

Carrie nodded while looking through the wooden floor of the bar. "You have no idea."

Chapter Six

Mornings were hard. Her evenings at the bar were becoming more and more frequent. And each time she was staying there later and later, and drinking more and more.

She reached over to her nightstand where she kept a ready supply of ibuprofen and always a glass of water. She popped three of the pills for good measure and took a tiny sip to wash them down. As she lay back down, the soft pillow even seemed to assault her. Just a few more minutes was all she needed to allow the pills to work.

Movement next to her roused her from her drift off back to sleep. She had forgotten about Simon and how, at the time last night, it had seemed like a good idea for him to bring her home.

She rolled over and out of her side of the bed and walked towards the bathroom. "Be gone when I get out of the shower," she said without looking back towards the bed.

The hot water washed away the stench of the night before. The booze, the sweat, the sex, all of it. Her hand tapped the faucet handle to tip the water even hotter as she rested her forehead against the tile. The near-searing heat cut through the pain of regret as she worked to stuff it all away.

Leaving the shower behind was hard, but it had done its job and she was once again alert and ready to start the day.

The reflection from the semi-clear swath her hand had cleared in the mirror fog looked unfamiliar. She stood staring at the Carrie she had become, was working to become. Someone who didn't feel the pain. No love, no pain.

Except for Melinda. That picture of the girl had activated something inside her and she still didn't know why. Caring for those she fought to save was essential in her line of work. She did however, struggle with how to find that line between caring enough to do a good job all while guarding her heart against pain. And then how to adhere to that line.

Since Simon had driven her home, she had to get her car from the bar. The short walk a few blocks away did her good, as much as she hated to admit it.

"You're late," said Randy as she walked through the door.

She pulled her sunglasses off and looked at her watch. "Five minutes." She looked back up and tilted her head slightly in challenge. Then she smiled. "Only five minutes. Give me a break." Her bravado was a front for the knot in her stomach. She was still relatively new here, and she needed to be a model agent.

Randy watched her. They had somewhat of a closeness, but he knew there was a lot that Carrie would not allow him to see in her life. What he could see was immensely complicated and in all honestly, she seemed to be in dire need of a therapist. But that was none of his business.

"Anything at all?" asked Carrie.

Randy knew she was referring to the two missing girls. "Nothing yet."

She had screamed until her voice was raspy. Now her body was convulsing with sobs over the futility of her situation.

Emily hated small spaces, and she was terrified having woken up in one. She could barely move, but she curled her fists and beat them down at her sides against the bottom of the box. She knew they were creating no sound to draw attention to her, but it expelled some of her fury.

How long had she been there? How long would it take her to die? How did she even get into this place?

She tried to retrace her steps for answers. She had been going to the neighborhood park. It was a great day, and she loved being outside. No one was there but her, which was fine. And that was all. Nothing else until she woke here in this box.

The sobbing started all over again, but the creaking of metal against metal halted her sobs. A face loomed in at her and she held her breath, waiting for the worst.

"Hi there. Now, who are you?" Emily didn't answer, her large blue eyes were fixed full and round.

"I'm Janet. Here, let me help you out of there." The lady extended one hand while holding the lid of the box open with the other. Still, Emily didn't move. "Are you hurt? Can you get out of there on your own?" Janet's face emphasized concern.

Finally, Emily moved and slowly sat up. Her body was still heaving from the hard crying, and she had exhausted herself. Her voice creaked as she asked, "Where am I?"

"Wow, sounds like you swallowed a frog there." Janet pushed the lid backwards in order to have both hands to help Emily. It landed on the ground with a dusty thud that startled her.

She shrunk back from the lady's touch but continued to work her way out of the box. Her hair and clothes were wet with sweat and tears, and the wind was blowing dust. She felt utterly miserable.

A scowl was fixed on her face as she glared at Janet. "I want to go home."

"Okay, okay. We'll see about that. But first, let's get you cleaned up and get some food and water in you." The woman was holding out her hand and motioning with her fingers to come towards her.

Emily was standing by the edge of the box looking at her surroundings while keeping a watch on Janet. She didn't trust her, even though she was grateful she had released her from the box. They were in a meadow next to a small stand of trees. There were no houses or any other signs of civilization that she could see.

She looked back at Janet, unsure about what to do. "I think I will just stay here for a while."

Janet dropped her hand and looked at Emily. Her smile faltered, but her demeanor wasn't threatening. "What if whoever put you in the box comes back? Do you want them to find you here?"

Emily's arms wrapped around herself, and she knew Janet was right. "Okay, I'll come. But I've got to get back home as soon as possible."

They walked for what seemed to be a very long time, through woods and meadows and up and down hills. "How far away are we?" Emily whined. The smell of the cow dung they were walking through wafted through the air and her tongue was so dry it was sticking to the roof of her mouth.

"Not too much further."

Suddenly, Emily's body plunged to the ground. "Ow!"

Janet turned swiftly back to see Emily's foot caught in an exposed tree limb. As she knelt to assess the situation, she could see her foot and ankle had already begun to swell and turn colors.

Emily was holding her knee up to her chest and was writhing back and forth, crying and screaming.

Janet hadn't thought about what to do if something like this happened. They were still quite a distance from her house and even though the girl was small, she knew she couldn't carry her that far.

Chapter Seven

A call came through from Matt Booker. "We found someone in Emily's neighborhood with a home video security feed. When we first canvased the area, they were not home. During a second round of door knocking we found them. They had just gotten back from vacation.

"They had just installed a new security system in their home. I'm going to send the feed over to you now. It shows Emily walking to the neighborhood park and swinging on the day she went missing."

Adrenaline rushed through Carrie's body, and she was instantly alert. She hovered over Randy's shoulder as he pulled up the feed. Home video surveillance technology, still being new, rendered a black and white and somewhat grainy picture. Fortunately, the house faced the park and the street in between. For several minutes, there was no activity. Then a car or two passed by the park before disappearing again from the screen.

"There!" Carrie nearly screamed in Randy's ear. He jumped and accidentally clicked the mouse to fast forward the feed. "Dammit, Carrie!"

"I'm sorry, but I saw her." She wanted to grab the mouse from Randy, who she was convinced was moving way too slow. Carrie stood and waited, her elbow resting on her other arm that was held against her stomach. She chewed on a fingernail and tapped her foot, growing more anxious by the second.

Finally, he had rewound the feed back to where Carrie had seen Emily appear. "There," Carrie whispered and pointed to the screen. Off to the far right, coming down the street that ran alongside the park and towards the house.

They could see Emily clearly as she walked towards the camera. She veered to her right, their left, and headed towards the swings. They could see no one else in or around the park. From the counter on the video, they knew Emily had been swinging for about ten minutes when someone approached her from behind. They wrapped their hands around her mouth and neck, dragging her backwards off of the swing.

She was small but didn't give in easily. She kicked her legs, and both hands grabbed the arm wrapped around her neck. The swings were to the far left of the screen and Emily was quickly dragged out of the view of the camera.

Hot anger overcame Carrie. She was furious. Furious at the kidnapper. Furious that they had so little to go on. Furious that she didn't know what to do next.

"Okay," said Randy. "We blow it up and see if we can get a closeup of the perp. It appears to be a man or a very large woman."

"They had a t-shirt hoodie on. I can't believe no one in the neighborhood saw them," said Carrie.

Randy was working to find the right still image to crop and zoom in. There was some type of picture on the front of the t-shirt, but blown up at this resolution, it was difficult to tell. There were only a few frames to capture it as the kidnapper was walking up behind Emily.

They finally chose one frame with what seemed to be the best facial image of the person. "Nothing. We can't tell anything from that," said Carrie. She walked away from the computer and Randy and began to pace the room.

After a few trips back and forth across the room, she glanced at Randy who was continuing to play the video over and over agian very slowly. "What are you doing?"

"Looking for anything unique about the subject. Tattoos or moles, anything that would set them apart from someone else." They both looked intently at the screen for the next several minutes, hyper focused on the image.

Nothing jumped out and as their eyes began to burn, Carrie shook her head to try and clear her exhausted mind. "Let's take a break and go add the info to the whiteboard," suggested Randy.

Carrie looked at the lack of information on the board as they walked into the room. She pushed despair aside, determined to focus her energy into what she was so good at. Carrie began pulling the pieces into her mind, imagining various scenarios, and living the event as if it were her.

Randy had seen her like this before. He stood quietly, watching her. Her mind was firing and making random connections. Most of those would amount to nothing, but some of the 'what-ifs' often contained the exact piece of information they needed.

She grabbed a clean white board and a marker and began to do what she called a brain dump. In a flurry, she wrote down as many potential scenarios that she could fit into these two abductions.

When she had finished, she capped the marker and stood back. "First, we have a human trafficking angle." She tapped the line with the capped marker and turned to look at Randy. When he didn't comment, she turned back to the board.

"I believe we can mark out any family-related motive. These two girls and their families didn't know each other. But there could be some weird link that we are not aware of.

"Should we mark it off?" She searched Randy's face as he assessed her thoughts on the board.

"I think we can. It would possibly be some kind of tit-for-tat agreement and that makes no sense."

Carrie uncapped the marker with a pop and drew a line through that thought.

"Serial killer," said Carrie. She stood thinking.

"If it is a serial killer, and it could be, I think we would have found a body. And the abductions have been pretty close together. No cooling off time."

"Unless these are not their first and they are escalating." They looked at each other as their minds attempted to probe each other's thoughts.

Finally, Carrie scrunched her face and said, "Naw, I don't think that fits." Instead of drawing a line through it, though, she just added two question marks beside it.

Then there was 'unrelated'. Randy shrugged. "They could be unrelated. Just a coincidence." His thoughts left hanging as his words drifted off.

"Neither of us believe in coincidences," said Carrie as she marked through the thought on the board.

Next was 'kidnapping.' "Usually kidnappings are for a single person with a targeted ransom demand. The only time I've seen multiples is when the two are together. Or there is a hostage situation that isn't really a kidnapping," said Randy.

"It is kidnapping, but the reason why is stumping us. Is it kidnapping for ransom, to keep for themselves, or...," and Carried drew a big red line and arrow back to her first thought, "kidnapping for human trafficking." Carrie tapped the board with the marker for emphasis.

"I hate to admit it, but it makes the most sense. Are they being sold off or are they being held hostage for prostitution?" asked Randy.

"That is what we have to find out."

"Hang on. I'll go get help." Janet's mind was racing. She couldn't go get a person. They would ask too many questions. But she could go get a cart she used to move stuff around the yard. Then worried that if she left the girl, someone else might happen upon her or that she might try to escape.

"Stay right here. I'll hurry."

Emily writhed in agony, but she kept her senses about her. She didn't know if she could walk, but as soon as the lady was out of eyesight, she would try.

Janet was a little too heavy and out of shape to run, but she walked as fast as she could back to her house. She had to stop every so often to hold the stitch in her side and breathe. This was all going wrong in so many ways.

Back at her house, she pulled her large garden cart from the shed and began walking back towards the girl. Just as she was about to leave the yard, she paused. She could at least take the girl some water, and maybe a quilt to sit on in the cart. She nodded to herself and went back to the house.

She found the items she meant to get, and threw in an Ace bandage for good measure. Walking was her only option back to the girl. There was no way she could hurry with this large cart. But she would try.

Thirty minutes later, Janet crested the hill, and she stopped. Her mind questioned if this was the place she had left her. She was almost certain it was. She panicked, realizing that the girl was gone. Either someone had taken her or she had gotten away.

She dropped the handles of the cart and took off running towards the empty spot where she had left the girl. Janet whirled frantically this way and that searching for any sign of Emily. There were none.

The ground showed swatches of displaced earth that looked like they could be drag marks. They were headed towards the woods. Janet's breathing slowed, and she inhaled deeply. She would find her and they would have a talk. Running off was not acceptable.

Janet's pace slowed as she walked in the direction of the thick pine trees in front of her. She was very unhappy that Emily had tried to run off. Maybe she wasn't as hurt as she had let on.

"Emily," Janet slowly called out as she stepped under the canopy of branches. The woods vegetation was spotty, growing thickly in many areas with other areas completely bare.

There was a lot of low growth that clustered around the bottoms of the trees. There were also briar vines that would cut a person to the quick if they weren't careful.

A rustle off to Janet's right caught her ear. But it was just a rabbit, scurrying away. "Emily. Come on now, honey. I have the cart and some water and a wrap for your ankle." She made sure to keep her voice low and non-threatening.

As Janet passed the spot where Emily was tucked in, the girl held her breath. The pain in her foot and ankle was almost unbearable, and she had made the unfortunate choice of cuddling next to the briars. It was all she could do to keep from crying out. She pinched her eyes tight, and focused on holding her breath as long as she could.

"There you are!" Janet's face suddenly popped into view. She had found her. Rivers of tears flooded Emily's eyes and, once again, sobs wracked her body.

Janet reached down and lifted the girl out of the bushes and, without a word, carried her to the cart.

Chapter Eight

Melinda was being well taken care of, but she was extremely suspicious of Peggy's procrastination in helping her find a phone or to get home.

After her shower, she had put on the clothes left by Peggy. They seemed out of style for a niece. They looked more like old lady clothes, but they were clean.

The jeans were loose and long, so she rolled up the hem. The shirt was a knit shirt she pulled over her head. It hung on her, shapeless. Melinda looked down and realized she was probably wearing some of Peggy's old clothes.

There was a hairbrush and toothbrush lying by the sink that looked clean, if not new. She picked up the brush and pulled it through her wet hair. She watched herself in the mirror and as she did, tears puddled in her eyes. When she could no longer see the mirror, she laid the brush down.

She knew something was wrong. But Peggy was being so nice and helpful. Her fists shoved the puddles away, and she looked around the room for her shoes. Where were they? Where had she left them? At first, she thought she was just not seeing them. Then her hair stood up at its roots as she realized they were not there and that Peggy had probably taken them.

She closed her eyes and forced herself to take a deep breath. Whatever was wrong, she would find out. She encouraged herself to be strong. Being smart about this would help her, and she was determined to outsmart that woman.

A noise outside the bathroom door brought Melinda back. "Are you doing okay in there?" Peggy asked.

"Yes. Just finishing up." Melinda reached for the doorknob and when she turned it, she felt the wobbly nature of the old knob. It was loose and rickety. Melinda again filed that information away as something that might help her later.

"I've made you lunch. I know you have to be hungry." Peggy's face beamed.

Melinda gave a slight nod and followed Peggy down the hallway. As she went, she tried to take in as much as she could and commit it to memory. The old wooden floors beneath her bare feet creaked and moaned as if warning her to beware. She would never sneak out of this place walking on these floors.

A small 1950s kitchen table and chairs sat as though it was waiting for a precious guest. The chairs were old, but there were no rips or tears in the turquoise vinyl. The center of the table had a white cotton table runner edged in a bit of crochet. It was starched.

The plates were pretty floral china, and cloth napkins were folded under the silverware. They were not actually silver, but very nice tableware nonetheless. A small clear vase of wildflowers sat in the middle of the setup.

"Pull out a chair. I don't get guests very often, so this is a treat." Peggy was fluttering around with nervous excitement.

Melinda did as she was told as Peggy turned to get a tray of food to bring to the table. The artfully-arranged food tray held various quartered sandwiches. There was also a selection of pickles, small carrots, celery and other raw vegetables. Also on the tray were two small bowls and spreaders. One with mustard and the other with mayonnaise.

Peggy moved the vase aside and sat the tray in the middle of the table. Melinda's stomach growled. "Oh, I knew you would be hungry," Peggy said when she heard it.

Instinct drew Melinda's hand across her stomach, as if to hold it back from betraying her further. "I guess I am," Melinda admitted.

She enjoyed lunch while simultaneously working out her escape plan. Finding her shoes was at the top of her priority list. It would be hard to run without them. Pavement would scorch her feet in the blistering sun, and goat heads and sand burs were everywhere here. She couldn't endure walking, or running in those.

Melinda took a sandwich quarter from the tray and looked at it to see what was in it. *Would she try to poison me*? But across the table, Peggy was placing several of the same type of sandwich sections onto her own plate. Melinda took a small bite and felt no immediate side effects. Being surprisingly good, she settled in to her small feast.

~

Carrie and Randy had sent the video to their forensic techs to see if they could enhance the front of the t-shirt hoodie. In the meantime, they had sat and gone through the video meticulously, stopping at each frame. When the suspect and Emily would exit the screen, Randy would then rewind and go back to the beginning.

After what seemed like the twentieth time, Randy leaned back in his chair with the video still running. Turning to look at Carrie, he said, "I can't look at that video any longer. My eyes are raw." Carrie nodded but was still watching the video roll. Her mind was searching for their next strategic step.

As she stared blankly at the screen, a car drove back down the street in between the house and the park. It had come from the direction that Emily had been taken. "Stop. Stop the video and go back."

She was frantically pointing at the monitor. Randy wheeled around and his hand flew back to his mouse. "Slow it down," Carrie unintentionally barked.

Randy allowed the screen to creep by as the 2002 Honda Civic came back into view. It was royal blue, and in the back there appeared to be a body-shaped form under a blanket. They backed the video up again and ran it forward. They zoomed in and out.

"I don't know," said Randy. "That could be anything. It could just be a pile of old clothes." He was tired and frustrated from staring at the screen all day.

"Well, the driver is wearing the same color hoodie as the abductor - that has to be Emily in the back!" Randy nodded in agreement and sent the clipped portion of the file to the tech team as well, to see what else they could determine.

Randy stood and stretched, and Carrie paced as she chewed on a nail. Her eyes appeared almost wild with thought. "What are you thinking?" Randy asked.

Carrie stopped and looked at him. "As soon as we get that close up of them with the tech enhancement and a pic of the car. We hit the streets and go to every house around that park. We'll knock on doors until we find someone, anyone, who saw that car. They may have been at the park other times too, waiting for the right child."

"Or they may have just been driving through and saw her."

"But just in case..."

"Sure, just in case," Randy agreed.

It only took the tech team one hour before getting back to them. The face was still grainy, but they were certain it was a man, probably between the ages of 25 and 35, 40 at the max. He had dark, thick hair and there was a small tattoo on his right hand near his thumb and index finger.

They zoomed in on the enhanced photo and thought the tattoo could be initials. Randy clicked print, and as soon as the photo shot out of the printer, he grabbed it and with a fine tipped Sharpie he carefully traced the tattoo. "NT. Very artistically done. Do you have your own initials done that pretty, or someone you love?" Randy asked.

"I would never have a tattoo of someone else on my body." Carrie's hard stare affirmed to Randy how deep her pain and distrust of others ran. "Sure. I know *you* wouldn't. But hypothetically, a normal person would probably only have initials this artistic of someone they loved tattooed on. Would anyone even tattoo their own initials on their own body at all?"

"Probably not."

"Someone may recognize the tattoo at any rate. We now have a car, a tattoo, a vague pic of the unsub, and a clear image of his pale blue t-shirt hoodie with an Eskimo Joe's logo on the front. It is enough to take door to door," Randy said, gathering the pics and file. "Let's hope for the best."

Chapter Nine

Riding in the cart to Janet's house was excruciating for Emily. The ground was rutted and Janet seemed to only be focused on getting there and not how they got there. The constant jostling and bumping jarred Emily, and pain continued to shoot through her ankle.

The cart was a garden cart and potting soil covered the bottom. Emily thought she could feel bugs or gnats coming up from the soil and crawling on her. But her misery hindered her desire to even care.

She glanced at her ankle, that was tilted upwards, resting on the rim of the cart. It was grotesquely swollen and purple. All she could do was close her eyes to shut her current situation out of her mind.

"We're here," Janet announced as she dropped the front end of the cart down, thrusting one last staccato shot of pain through Emily's body.

Janet walked to the side of the cart and looked down at Emily. Her hands rested on her hips and she wondered what to do with the girl. This is not how things were supposed to go.

Seeing the girl lay there, disheveled and dirty with gnats crawling all over her, Janet was suddenly moved to compassion. "Here, let me get you inside so we can tend to you," she said as she once again scooped Emily out of the cart and carried her towards the house.

Emily had no more fight left in her, so she simply relaxed in the woman's arms and rested her head on Janet's chest as she was carried away. She feared the worse, but was exhausted and in too much pain to fight any more.

Janet carried Emily up the steps to the front deck of her mobile home. The door was always unlocked. There was no need to lock it so far away from civilization. Inside, the AC window unit was struggling to keep up as the sun bore down on the tin structure.

Emily felt herself being gently lowered to what seemed to be the living room sofa. The fabric was prickly and stiff. *One more irritant to endure.*

"Let me look at that wound." Janet moved down to Emily's ankle. In an attempt to assess the situation, she carefully turned her foot. Emily screamed in agony.

"I think it is broken," she sobbed. "Don't touch it." She feared the woman would never take her to a doctor. She suspected she was this woman's captive and that she would never go home. And now, with this broken ankle, there was no way she could even try to get away. She wished she had just died in that box.

~

Randy and Carrie had knocked on the doors of six houses that surrounded the park. It was a workday and most occupants were gone.

"Should we wait and come back after they are home from work?" Carrie asked Randy.

He stood with one hand on his hip and a clipboard in the

other. They had a list of every address and homeowner that surrounded the park. He looked around as they stood in the yard of the next house on their list. The neighborhood was quiet and there was no one outside of the houses or in the park.

"Let's keep going. If we find anyone at all, then that will shorten our list. Besides, Emily was taken around this time of day, so if anyone was home, then they might be home today as well."

As they turned toward the house, Carrie saw movement in the front window. The curtain was still barely swinging from being dropped back into place.

"Someone is home here," Carrie said as she nodded towards the swinging curtain.

Randy knocked on the door, and they listened for a response. There was no sound of footsteps or movement that they could detect inside.

Again, Randy knocked. "I am Randy Jeffries with the Oklahoma State Bureau of Investigation. Please answer the door."

"Maybe it's a kid home for the summer while the parents work. They have most likely been told to not answer the door," Carrie said.

"True."

"We are law enforcement. If your parents have told you not to answer the door while home alone, we understand. But we need to talk just a minute. If you open the door just a crack, we will step back off of the porch to talk."

The curtain moved again just slightly. A small eye peered through the slit between the wall and curtain. Randy stepped back off of the porch and held up his badge. Carrie joined him and they stood patiently, waiting.

The eye surveyed the badge for what seemed like a very long time. Were they deciding what to do? Neither Carrie nor Randy knew.

But then there was a slight rattle at the door. The deadbolt slid back, and the doorknob turned. The same eye that had watched them from the window now watched them from the crack in the door.

"My parents aren't home, and I am not supposed to answer the door when they are gone."

"We understand," said Randy. "I wouldn't want my children to answer the door either. But we really need some help and maybe you can help us. You can stay there."

"Okay."

"Are you home most days? Did you happen to notice this car at the park earlier this week?" Randy held up an 8x10 of the blue Civic.

The door swung open a few more inches to reveal a young boy of about twelve. He studied the picture and then looked Randy right in the eye and nodded an affirmative.

"Was it parked or driving?"

"It was parked over there." The boy pointed to the parking spot nearest the swings.

"Did you see this girl in the park playing on the swings?" Randy held up the picture of Emily that her parents had given them.

With barely seeing the picture, the boy nodded. "She comes to the park a lot."

"Now this is very very important. Did you see the man who was driving this blue car?"

The boy's brow dipped as he thought. He looked down at the front porch and then he looked up and nodded. Randy hated to rush him, but he was feeling an urgency to pull all he could out of the boy.

"Did you see this man take this girl from the park and put her in his car?"

The boy took a step back into the house, and the door began to close. "No, wait, please don't go. You are okay. No one is going to harm you. Please." Carrie pleaded with the boy.

Without the door opening back up, the boy pressed his face to the opening. "I saw him take her." Then he was suddenly gone, and the door closed to the sound of the deadbolt sliding shut.

Carrie and Randy didn't know whether or not to be relieved. "We know from the list who his parents are. We can come back when they are home," said Carrie.

Randy was nodding as he wrote down all that the boy had said.

"Do you think he is afraid?" Carrie asked.

Randy continued to write in silence so he wouldn't forget anything as Carrie waited. When he raised his pen, he said, "No doubt. He looks to be about her age. If he stays home by himself every day and he saw that man abduct Emily, then he is probably terrified."

"Do you think he even told his parents?" Carrie asked.

"I don't know. Depends on what his parents are like." Randy could feel that they were still being watched behind the curtain, and he held up his hand and waved with a smile. The curtain fell back into place and stayed there.

Chapter Ten

Eskimo Joe's apparel in Oklahoma was as plentiful as were windy days there. The iconic eatery in the college town of Stillwater was incredibly popular even if you never attended Oklahoma State University. Nearly everyone had something with that logo on it at one time or another.

Finding the person wearing a logoed light blue t-shirt hoodie seemed overwhelming. He could have bought it, or it could have been a gift. Shoot, for that matter, he could have borrowed it.

Carrie sat at her desk and stared at the picture of the man who had taken Emily. She was trying to force her mind, which had been professionally trained for such situations, to perform at will. She just didn't have enough to go on.

"We got a partial plate on the blue Civic. The tech team was able to enhance the still enough to get the first few letters. Still not enough." Randy plopped down in his chair and began sifting through the file yet again.

Carrie watched him. They had proven to make a good team. He was laser focused and didn't move rashly. Carrie tended to jump and run, but he held her back with common sense and caution. She often spurred him on with her creative, out-of-the-box thinking. She was glad they had partnered her with Randy.

"So, is there enough to get a list at least?" Carrie asked.

"I ran it. Over 500 Honda Civics in OKC alone with those tag numbers. They are the first letters, which is Oklahoma county, then a 5. Not much at all to go on." Randy exhibited the discouragement that Carrie felt.

"But at least we have the boy," Carrie said.

Randy looked up and nodded. "I hope that with a thorough interview, if his parents allow it, we will get something usable."

Carrie nodded in response. "Did you reach them yet?"

"Yes. We have an appointment to meet with them at 6:00 pm this evening."

"Lunch was good. Thank you." Melinda knew she would get more out of Peggy if she were kind and respectful.

"You are welcome." Peggy beamed back at the girl, almost amazed at her kindness. She had expected more pushback.

"So, now that I've gotten cleaned up, eaten, and rested, how do we go about contacting my parents?" Melinda asked.

A sinking feeling instantly replaced the joy that Peggy had just felt. She had hoped too soon. "Well, as I said, we are a long way from town."

"But you do go to town, don't you?" Melinda asked. Each word carried a slightly sharp delivery.

"Not often." Peggy's nervous giggle didn't prove to alleviate Melinda's fears.

"But this is not any ordinary situation. When you need to get to town, when you HAVE to get to town, how do you get there?" Melinda was trying to not lose control, but she was growing tired of the runaround.

"I have an old truck in the barn, but it isn't running right now."

Melinda's eyes narrowed. "What do we need to do to get it running?"

"I've ordered a part. But it is back ordered. I'm just waiting for it to come."

"How did you order the part?" Melinda was sharp witted and was going to trap Peggy in a lie if she could. She knew she risked angering her, but she didn't care. At this point, she didn't believe anything that the woman had told her. "You don't have a phone, or so you've said, so how did you order the part?"

Peggy was getting nervous. "Mail order. I took the order form from the parts book and mailed it in." She was wringing her hands which were becoming blotchy and red.

Melinda crossed her arms and looked straight into Peggy's eyes. "That is bullshit! I don't believe a word you are saying. I won't let you keep me here. I will walk 60 miles if I have to in order to get to the nearest town." Melinda's controlled anger set Peggy back.

"No, no. Please don't go." Peggy was afraid the plan was all falling apart. She needed Melinda to want to stay with her. If she treated her kindly and took care of her well, she was convinced she would want to stay. She reached out towards Melinda, who backed up. The look of disdain on her face made Peggy's heart crumble. All she had wanted was a child to love.

Peggy ran to the front door and locked it. She turned around and stood with her back to the door, guarding it. "Please, just give me some more time."

Melinda stood, assessing the situation. She knew the back door was to her right. She could run to the kitchen and out that door. She didn't think it was locked. Her experience in sports had kept her fit. She knew she could outrun Peggy, but Peggy was larger and could overpower her if they engaged in a physical battle.

"Okay, okay." Melinda decided to play along for a bit,

switching gears until she could get away and run. Her body relaxed and as a result, so did Peggy's. "I need a nap. All of this has made me tired."

Peggy's head was nodding rapidly. She had almost lost the girl and needed to find a way to make the girl trust her, but how? She vowed to love her so much that she would never want to leave.

"Here, I have the perfect room for you." Peggy ushered Melinda down the hall and into a sweet room full of light from the windows.

Melinda stood and looked around. As was the rest of the house, it was clean and tidy. The walls were painted pink and the curtains and bedspread were floral and ruffly. She had only seen this old-fashioned stuff in the catalogs her grandmother still received in the mail.

She picked up one of the large, deep ruffles that surrounded the edge of the bedspread. It was a thin, sheer nylon with large pink flowers. No one her age would ever want something like this. She dropped it and turned to Peggy. "It is so pretty. Thank you." As she turned back away to lie down, the smile transformed into anger. She would play Peggy's game and she would win.

~

"I have to touch it. I will be gentle. I promise." The ankle was so swollen that it frightened Janet. She knew Emily was probably right, and that her ankle was broken and not just sprained.

"It needs to be wrapped. I have a bandage. I'll wrap it and put ice on it. If we do that and elevate it, it will begin to heal."

Emily just laid there. Her head ached from all the screaming and crying. She felt so foggy that conversation was not possible. She simply closed her eyes once again to shut out the horrible woman.

Janet hurried off to her kitchen and began accumulating

supplies. Emily heard water splashing into some type of container. Janet then appeared with a towel over her shoulder and a square tub filled with water, which she set down beside the sofa on the ugly shag carpet.

She scurried back to grab the supplies she had pulled from the cabinets and returned. "Here. Let me wash your foot and ankle."

Emily was lying on her side with the leg of her hurt foot straight out on top. Her other leg was bent underneath, supporting it.

Janet carefully lifted the hurt leg to push a dry towel underneath the foot, and laid it back down. Emily's body had tensed in anticipation of more sharp pain from the movement. But it proved to be not much worse than she was already enduring. She knew Janet was trying to not hurt her, but she didn't care, she remained furious at the woman.

She heard Janet dip something into the water and wring it out. Again, she tensed in anticipation of the painful touch. Janet barely rested a wet cloth onto Emily's foot, slowly dragging it across from toes to ankle.

The cool water felt good, and Emily relaxed. When Janet had done all that she could do in that position, she once again lifted her leg and used the same technique to wash the underside.

"I think I have it clean. But now I need to wrap it. I'm afraid that this might hurt some," said Janet. Emily merely nodded with her eyes still closed and braced herself for the coming pain.

Janet lifted Emily's foot and began wrapping the ankle. It hurt, but when she was done, Emily thought it actually felt much better.

"Okay. Now we need to elevate it and get some ice on it." Janet was already taking the tub of water back to the kitchen. Sounds of the freezer opening and ice being moved about was all Emily heard.

"Can you turn over onto your back?" Janet asked as she returned.

Emily slowly did as she was told, with as little exertion as possible. Janet raised the leg high and placed a large fluffy bed pillow under her foot. It was now throbbing, which added to Emily's discomfort.

Janet had a ziplock baggie of ice, but hesitated before attempting to lay it on the ankle. She knew that the weight of the ice would hurt. "I have to get this ice on there. It may be a bit heavy."

All Emily could do was give her a slight nod. But again, Janet was careful and held the bag so that it touched her ankle without putting the full weight of it down.

Soon the cold seeped through Emily's ankle, and exhaustion carried her away to sleep.

Chapter Eleven

The boy's parents were waiting for Carrie and Randy. As soon as they stepped onto the porch, the door swung open and two very concerned faces greeted the agents.

"Hello. We are agents Jeffries and Border. Thank you for meeting with us this evening," said Randy as the couple ushered them into the cozy living room.

They were seated on an oversized sofa, which threatened to suck them in. Mrs. Peterson then asked if they wanted something to drink, but both agents declined.

"So, you wanted to talk to us about an abduction in the park?" Both parents sat on facing chairs, leaning intently towards the agents with creased brows.

Randy explained what he could to bring them up to speed without revealing classified information. When he got to the part where they had spoken with their son earlier in the day, surprise and then growing anger registered on their faces.

Randy said quickly, "Please don't be angry with your son. He handled everything very well. He refused to open the door until he saw the badge and then he opened it only a crack to talk with us.

We agreed to step back, completely off of the porch for his comfort.

"But he saw the abduction. Once he confirmed that, he went back into the house, so we left. We knew at that point that we needed to interview him further with you present." Randy left his last statement to hang in the air so that the Petersons, could soak it in.

They looked at each other, both deep in thought. Mr. Peterson finally nodded sharply at Randy and rose to go get their son Alexander. He didn't have to go far. The boy was a quiet shadow just behind the door into the next room.

The boy was scared. That was clear to everyone. He hung close to his father, who they could tell made Alexander feel safe. Too big to sit on his father's lap in the chair, he stood beside him with his arms crossed.

"Hi Alexander..." Randy began.

"Alex," the boy quickly corrected.

"Alex." Randy accepted the correction with a smile and continued. "You told us earlier that you saw this car earlier this week and the man who was driving it." Randy paused for confirmation. He received it as a nod from Alex.

"What can you tell us about the man?"

Alex's eyes searched the room and his parents' faces. "I don't know."

Randy knew he needed to break through the tension. "Okay. Well, I know that sometimes we know more than we remember at first. What if we get you a chair and you can relax a bit?"

With raised questioning eyebrows, Randy rose and moved to a chair that was sitting on the far side of the wall. The couple quickly nodded, answering his silent question. Randy moved the wooden chair into their circle, making sure to leave it closer to Alex's father than to theirs. But he did strategically face it right towards him.

Alex sat and looked by design towards Randy. "When you saw the man take the girl, what did you think at the time?"

Alex gave a slight shake of his head and shrugged his shoulders as if he didn't want to discuss the matter.

"Look, I know it isn't something that is pleasant to talk about. You aren't in any kind of trouble and you have nothing to be afraid of. I just want you to relax and think about that day.

"What were you doing before you looked out the window?"

Alex looked down at the colorful area rug. "I was coming downstairs to turn on the TV and I heard the swings. They creak when someone is swinging. I stopped and looked out and saw the girl. She comes to the park a lot. I stood there watching her because I wanted to go out there with her, but knew I would get in trouble for leaving the house.

"Then the blue car pulled up. It was going real slow, and I don't think she heard it coming. He got out and walked up behind her. He pulled her off of the swing and shoved her in his backseat. I dropped the curtain. He looked up. I don't know if he saw me or not."

"Okay, okay. That is good Alex. You are doing very good." Randy spoke in a soothing voice, a technique he knew would help to calm anxiety in an interrogation. "What can you tell me about the man himself? What did he look like and what was he wearing?"

"He had dark hair, kind of full and a little bushy. And a mustache too. He was wearing an Eskimo Joe's hoodie. You know, one of those t-shirt ones, but it had long sleeves."

"That is excellent, Alex. Did he wear glasses or have any tattoos or anything else that you can remember?"

"No glasses. I didn't see any tattoos." Alex sat for a minute, thinking. Randy wanted to give him time, so they sat quietly. Finally, Alex just shrugged and shook his head. "That's all I guess."

"Okay. What about the girl? When he put her into the backseat. Did you see him do anything else to her?" Alex seemed to be breathing a bit slower now, as he furrowed his brow in concentration.

"He had put a rag over her mouth when he pulled her off of the swing," he said slowly, pausing as he seemed to recall more detail from the incident. "When he had her in the car, he took it off and it looked like she was asleep. He put some tape over her mouth. That silver tape like dad has. He put tape around her wrists too." Alex held out his hands with his wrists pushed together to demonstrate.

"He pushed her all the way in and covered her with a blanket or quilt or something. Then when he was standing back up, that is when he looked straight at our house. I don't know if he saw me or not," Alex repeated, agitated once again.

"My guess is he didn't see you. Do you think you could sit with our guy back at the tech lab and see if he can create a picture of the man based on your description?"

"Would I get to come to where all the cops are?" Alex brightened.

Randy chuckled and said, "Well, we are not cops. We are state investigative agents, but yes, you will be there with the agents. We can even give you a quick tour of our facilities if you like."

That prospect buoyed Alex. They made arrangements for one of the parents to bring Alex to the office the next day.

Back on the porch as the front door closed, they both stood looking toward the park. "He was so close to Alex. He parked the car right there. No wonder he was so frightened," Carrie said.

"Let's hope I was right, and he didn't see the kid. We don't need another missing child on our hands, and one that might have to pay for watching the perpetrator in action."

Melinda was exhausted. All the adrenaline from her ordeal had completely dissipated and left her nearly useless. She had taken a long nap and once awake, continued to lie on the bed. She still did not know where she was or how far away from help she was.

If Peggy wanted to keep her from leaving, then she had probably also lied about their location and the distance from town. Melinda didn't believe for one second that Peggy's truck was broken down or that she had ordered a part to fix it herself.

A golden red glow in the window signaled the setting sun, and that Melinda had napped much longer than she had intended, but she had needed the rest. She would need to stay awake longer tonight to escape, so she was glad she had slept.

The floor creaked in the hallway and Melinda knew Peggy was sneaking around, trying to see if she was awake. With her back to the door, Melinda knew Peggy couldn't see if her eyes were open or not. She shut them again.

A slight tap at the door. "Melinda, are you still asleep?" Peggy spoke just above a whisper. She hoped the girl was awake, but also didn't want to wake her if she still needed her rest. She also hoped that when Melinda woke, she would be in a better mood and more willing to spend time with Peggy.

Melinda took a deep breath of resolve and turned to see Peggy at the door. She saw that tension drew Peggy's body into a tight string that resonated on her face. It was clear that she was concerned about what she would do and that made Melinda smile inside. She had the upper hand.

"I just woke up."

Melinda moved to sit up, swinging her feet to the floor and standing. She faced Peggy and watched her nervousness. *What is the full story here? How had I come to be in the box? And how had Peggy become my rescuer?*

"Would you like to come out to the living room?"

Melinda nodded and moved towards the door. Peggy had

become very careful to make sure that Melinda was ahead of her when the moved down the hall. When Melinda challenged her earlier, caution surged through Peggy and she found she didn't trust Melinda to follow behind her.

Once in the living room, Peggy motioned for Melinda to sit in a chair with yet another floral print. It had crocheted doilies on the arms and she ran her fingers across them. They were a curious thing to Melinda.

"Do you like those?" Peggy asked brightly. Maybe they could connect through crochet.

"They look like someone worked hard to make them." Melinda would not admit to liking them because she couldn't say that. But she could see that they had been a labor of love for someone.

"Yes. But it doesn't seem like hard work anymore. I enjoy it and it has become easy for me. Maybe I could teach you."

Melinda saw hope on Peggy's face. Whatever she needed to do to play the game, bide her time, she would.

"Yeah, sure. That would be nice," Melinda said half-heartedly.

Chapter Twelve

Carrie's attempt at moderation with drinking and sex was to set a schedule. She made a vow to herself that she would only go to the bar every other night. A couple of years ago, it had gotten completely out of hand and she found herself at the bar nearly every night.

Her home was an easy place to entice a willing victim to come home with her, so she would not have to be alone. The first thing the next morning, though, she rudely made them leave. It was her house, and she was done with them, so she made no bones about it being time for them to leave.

There wasn't any chance of developing emotional attachments since she could barely remember the previous evening or what had happened once she had brought them home. She told herself that was exactly the way she wanted it.

Pain of loss had previously cut her so deep and so wide that she had convinced herself recovery would never come. And she wasn't sure she wanted it to come. There was a sense of safety behind the formidable emotional wall she had built. It was meant to guarantee she would never hurt like that again.

Tonight was a non-bar night. She and Randy had stayed at the Peterson's home until seven p.m. and it was now nearly eight. Carrie felt old, even though she was only twenty-eight. Her small home served as both a respite and also a cold reminder of what she had lost. The emptiness often echoed with the laughter she and Billy had shared, and the reminder of why it had all stopped.

Tossing her keys in the small bowl on the table by the door, she then dropped her purse to the floor. She unclipped her gun and took it to her bedroom to put it away for the night. She had a compact single gun safe that fit nicely in the top drawer of her nightstand, and she placed her gun there.

A rumble in her stomach reminded her she needed to eat, whether or not she wanted to. She chided herself for not driving through somewhere on her way home. She knew her cupboards were relatively bare, and she mainly used the fridge for beer.

Once changed into a comfortable pair of pjs, she went to the kitchen and began opening cabinet doors. Just as she thought, nothing.

The fridge yielded little more, but it did hold a gleaming six-pack of Michelob Light that beckoned to her. The internal debate was on. She really needed to eat, and she knew that once she slid one of those amber bottles out of its cardboard slot, she wouldn't eat a bite. She shut the door and picked up her phone.

"Yeah, it's Carrie. Send me my usual? Yep, same card that you have on file. Thanks Sam." They knew her by heart at the local Dominoes. She shuddered to think how many nights a week they had supplied her with at least a semblance of nutrition.

While she waited, she got out her notebook and read over the meager notes she had made. Randy usually took all the notes, and Carrie just listened. She had learned in college that she learned better by listening and focusing on the one speaking, committing it to memory right then and there. But later, once they had left, she had jotted down a few thoughts that had come to mind.

If it is human trafficking then we need to get with the OKCPD task force charged with all things in that realm. They would know who to talk to and they might have a lead that we haven't thought of.

A knock on the door snapped Carrie from her thoughts and soon she was sitting with the pizza box on the coffee table and a bottle in her hand, her secret comforts. Soon she felt full and buzzed and drifted off to sleep on the sofa with Jimmy Fallon in the background.

~

Emily woke to throbbing pain. Groggy from sleeping so hard, she didn't know where she was or what had happened. Just for a moment though, because the pain in her ankle quickly thrust her back to the full truth of her situation.

She raised her head to see her ankle still resting on the pillow and wrapped in an Ace bandage. Her toes were jutting out like little purple sausages. Her leg above the bandage was equally discolored and swollen.

Janet seemed to be nowhere around. The bandage needed to be loosened, but Emily didn't know if she could do it herself. Any movement at all sent excruciatingly painful throbs up her entire leg.

Through short controlled movements she finally maneuvered herself where she could reach the safety pin Janet had used to secure the bandage in place. As soon as Emily was able to release the pin, the bandage shrank back, releasing the pressure it had been forced to hold on her foot. Relief was instant and Emily lay back on the sofa.

With the bandage released now, the pain was sharp and cutting. She knew she needed to put the bandage back on, but she had to rest for a moment. It seemed her body was in rebellion against her at the moment, and forcing it to move seemed impossible.

Footsteps produced Janet at her side. "The bandage is off."

"It was too tight. I needed to loosen it. I know it needs to be put back on, but not so tight." Emily looked up with pleading eyes at Janet.

"Oh okay. Yes, I can see that. I'll do that for you. Where did the ice pack go?" Janet looked around the pillow and saw that it had fallen into the crevice between the pillow and sofa back once the ice had melted.

"Let me get your foot wrapped again and I'll get you more ice." Janet once again wrapped Emily's ankle, checking from time to time to make sure she wasn't wrapping it too tight. "It needs to be just a bit tight so that it holds it steady and secure."

Emily was so disengaged from the despair she felt that she didn't even bother to answer. How would she ever get out of this situation? Tears slid down the side of her face. As they puddled in her ear, she irritably wiped them away.

Janet left and came back into the room with another bag of ice and gently laid it on her ankle. It hurt, but Emily sucked in her breath and held it to withstand the pain.

"I need to go to the hospital."

Janet stood and looked down at Emily. She could tell the girl was miserable, but there was no way she could take her anywhere. Unable to give her the answer she wanted to hear, she simply turned and walked away.

"Did you hear me?" Emily half yelled in the direction Janet had walked.

When no response came, Emily then screamed in utter frustration. "Did you hear me? I need to go to a hospital!" When no sound came, Emily broke down sobbing. When the worst of the tears subsided, Emily said quietly, with her now raspy voice, "Can you at least help me get to the toilet?"

The man sat and looked at the girls walking from the dance studio. They seemed to be about the right age, but none fit the criteria on the latest list he had received. He looked down at the piece of notepaper with crudely written details.

Red hair was at the top of the list. When the last of the girls had gone and the parking lot was empty, he turned his key and left.

He drove around for the next several hours, looking. There was one redhead, but she was much too old. This project was much harder than he thought it would be. The money had seemed good at first, real good. On the surface, it seemed like easy money, but that was proving not to be the case.

Being a metal fabricator and welder for years made making the boxes easy. They needed to be airtight except for the lid. That would have the slightest margin for air to seep in and out, but not light. The captives had to believe someone had trapped them underground with diminishing air. That way, when they were found, they would be so grateful to the person rescuing them it would bond them to their rescuer. From then it was up to the rescuers to grow that bond so the girls would want to stay.

The whole thing seemed twisted to him, but he was in it for the money. Gratitude was one thing, but a young child would never be so grateful to someone for rescuing them that they would want to stay, unless their own family was abusive, and even then it was questionable.

Then suddenly, a flash of copper hair caught his eye. A young girl about eleven was walking on the sidewalk. She had long hair that was fashioned in a French braid that fell down her back nearly to her waist. She was on the smaller side and had a slight dusting of freckles across her nose. Above them flashed bright green eyes.

The man stayed back far enough so that she wouldn't notice him or grow suspicious. He would watch her and bide his time. Soon enough, he would know where and when was the best time to strike.

Chapter Thirteen

The next morning, Carrie arrived before Randy. It seemed strange; he was always early. Carrie logged into her computer while waiting for him to see what the plan was for the day. Nothing new from the tech team in her inbox, so she decided she would work on the list of blue Honda Civic owners.

An hour later, she had only gotten a fraction of the way through the list. This kind of grunt work bored Carrie. She would much rather be out pounding the streets than behind her desk.

She looked up and Randy's desk still sat empty. *Where is he?* She made her way to SAC Bracket's office and leaned her head around the corner. "I'm sorry to bother you, but Randy hasn't come in yet this morning. Do you know why?"

Bracket looked up and smiled at Carrie. He motioned for her to come in and sit in one of the chairs facing his desk.

"Randy went with Sandy to a doctors appointment this morning. He should be here soon."

Carrie didn't like the sound of that. Plus, she cared about them. "Is there anything to be concerned about?" Carrie asked.

Seeing the look on Carrie's face, Bracket quickly said, "No, not at all. Just something routine. But he wanted to be there with her."

"I see," replied Carrie.

"So, while we have some time here, tell me how you are doing, Carrie."

"I'm fine. I love it here. It's great working with Randy."

"But how are you doing?" There had been a few troubling signs of what Bracket assumed was Carrie's personal life, but didn't know for a fact. He knew her situation from the beginning and had seen how she had grown deeper into herself, shutting herself off emotionally since he had first met her.

Carrie slapped on a bit of brightness to her countenance and said, "Oh, I'm doing great." She would never want Bracket to know how she really was. Her highest priority was to not allow her personal disfunction to bleed over to her work life, which in all honesty was often hard to do.

"Good. So, how is the case coming?"

"Oh, that is a different story. It seems so slow going." Carrie continued to discuss with SAC Bracket all the evidence they had and what they had been doing. She told him about the boy and their plans to continue to canvas the neighborhood.

"I also thought that maybe if we are dealing with a human trafficking ring, then the OKCPD task force on that issue might have some leads. But I was waiting for Randy to come in to discuss it with him."

"Discuss what with Randy?" Carrie whirled around to see Randy standing in the doorway. He was beaming from ear to ear.

Bracket stood. "Well?"

"We're pregnant and it's due in six months!"

Carrie was dumbstruck. The thought had never crossed her mind. "Wow. That's great," she said, wishing she could feel the emotions that her words should have carried. She was happy for Randy. Really, she was. He was expanding his family and adding more people to love into his life. While all Carrie wanted to do was block out anyone she might love in an effort to eliminate any chance of pain.

Carrie stood watching Randy and Bracket slap each other on the back and talk excitedly about Randy's expanding family. She was a bystander on the sidelines, feeling hollow and alone.

~

Peggy had been so overjoyed that Melinda wanted to learn to crochet that she quickly brought out her stash of crochet threads, yarns, and crochet hooks.

Melinda wasn't in the mood for this. She didn't even know how long she had been gone from home. She knew they would look for her, but would they know to look for her two states to the north? She didn't think so.

She tried to focus on the instructions Peggy was so carefully giving, but her mind kept slipping to her situation and how she might escape it.

"You're not paying attention," Peggy burst forth from frustration.

"I'm sorry. I'm trying. Everything is just so new to me, and I am worried about my parents. I know they must be missing me."

Peggy calmed down and sat looking at the girl. She had known this wouldn't be easy, and she sympathized with the parents, but Peggy had never married. No one had ever wanted her, so she could never have a child.

With no family to take care of, she had spent years putting her hard-earned money in savings. She had inherited the house and land, so she only had taxes and insurance to pay on the property and her low utility bills. Her savings had grown considerably through the years and when she stumbled on this opportunity, she readily dumped tens of thousands of dollars into it, hoping for a child to love.

The money would get her a child, but it was up to her to love them enough for them to want to stay. Peggy was convinced she could.

"I know. I'm sorry. Maybe the crocheting will help you take your mind off of it. I'll go slower."

Melinda nodded and fixed her mind on the task of looping the yarn around the little metal hooked tool and pulling it through one loop after another. Soon she settled into the rhythm of the process, and it did feel like a soothing distraction, at least for now.

After a couple of hours of crocheting lessons, Melinda dropped her hands to her lap. She sat back in the plush chair and rubbed her eyes, and watched Peggy work on what appeared to be squares in bright colors. She remembered her saying something about putting them together to make an afghan.

"So, Peggy, tell me about yourself."

A symphony of emotions fought for control over Peggy's face in such a rapid succession that Melinda wasn't sure what was going to surface. Then finally Peggy looked at Melinda with a sad look. "My story isn't interesting." Her voice was so quiet that Melinda barely heard her.

Melinda leaned forward with her arms resting on her thighs. "It would be interesting to me." At that moment, she felt compassion for the woman and her comment had been birthed from sincerity.

"Really?" The barest flicker of hope crossed Peggy's face. No one had cared about her or her story, ever. *Could it be possible that this girl really does care about me?*

"Of course. Have you always lived on a farm? Do you have brothers and sisters?" Melinda watched as Peggy searched for the words she wanted Melinda to hear. It was difficult because without a filter, she would spew forth the bitterness that had brought her to this moment. To this place where she was reduced to hiring thugs to kidnap a child for her to love. But she couldn't let Melinda see that part of her.

"I grew up on this farm. I didn't have any brothers or sisters. My dad farmed from sunup to sunset. He was kind, but not the type to be affectionate, if you know what I mean." Peggy looked at Melinda to gauge her response so far. All was well, so she continued. "My mother was a stay-at-home mom and we lived off of what the farm produced, so she was continually cooking and canning, cleaning too. I had to help her tend the garden."

"Did you enjoy that? Being close to your mother in that way?"

"I never thought of it as being close. I was there with her, doing things that needed to be done, but there wasn't much camaraderie. Not much conversation. I think she had a hard life. A lot of work and no life away from here." Peggy stopped, lost in remembering.

"As I look back on it, I think she must have been very sad. I think they both were." Peggy's voice drifted away as she reconsidered her parents in a way she never had before.

From the time she had been a child, she was angry that her life was not better, different. She blamed her parents internally, and that discontent grew and festered. As she became an adult, she never stopped to think about the bitterness she carried. She never once asked herself if that bitterness had been justified, or just a childish misconception.

"That must have been difficult for them to have had to work so hard on the farm." Melinda's voice shifted Peggy's thoughts away from her contemplation. She looked up at the girl with fresh eyes and sat pondering her words as a new understanding overwhelmed her.

Then finally Peggy responded, "Yes, Melinda. I think you are right. Life must have been very hard for them. I think they must have tried to be good parents, but then life seemed so hard for them." This new revelation cracked the blanket of bitterness she had formed around her heart. Love poked its resilient head through the crack and she felt something she hadn't felt in decades.

As love for her parents seeped through and took over, regret came like a dagger. Regret from wasted years and wasted anger. Regret that she had not loved her parents the way they had deserved to be loved and now it was too late.

Melinda sat quietly. She knew Peggy had forgotten about her completely. She could tell the woman's mind was living inside itself, replaying memories that were quite painful. First one tear, then another, flowed over ruddy cheeks and dripped from her chin.

Peggy finally looked up at Melinda through tear-soaked eyes. *What has just happened to her?* Melinda wondered. In a split second, everything had changed.

How it had happened or why it had happened was a mystery, but Peggy felt as though everything she had thought she knew had been brought into question. Suddenly, she realized that the motives that had driven every day of her adult life were so incredibly wrong and had sprouted from her own deceived and selfish heart.

The girl before her was a beautiful girl. Peggy saw her for the first time. Really saw her. She had dark hair that hung past her shoulders and her green eyes were a vivid green, so rare she thought. There was a compassion about her and it drew Peggy to feel compassion in return.

This girl had parents who loved her and they must be terrified. What had she done? The reality of it came crushing in and it nearly sucked the life from her.

"I have to get you home."

Melinda's brows dipped as the reality sank in. She had suspected that Peggy was dragging her feet to delay the inevitable, but never dreamed that she had intended to keep her permanently.

Chapter Fourteen

All the fight had gone out of Emily. Despair had taken its place, and she lay despondent on the old sofa. Janet had given her some ibuprofen, which had barely touched the pain. She knew if they did not properly take care of her ankle, her days of playing softball were over. At this moment, though, she didn't even know if she would be alive to enjoy anything ever again.

"How are you?" Janet bounced into the room with a mixture of elation and nervous energy. It thrilled her to have the girl, but she was concerned about her ankle and her unwillingness to engage.

"Fine," Emily barely responded. She despised the woman, and wished she would just leave her alone and let her die.

"Are you comfortable?" Janet asked.

Was this stupid woman serious? She felt anger flush through her and she couldn't let the asinine comment go by. She raised up on one elbow so she could spit her venomous words at her captor in the way that she felt it.

"How stupid are you? No, I'm not comfortable. You have taken me captive and you won't get me medical help. I lay on this stinking old rat-infested sofa with my ankle screaming in pain. No, I'm not frickin' comfortable!" Emily's words bit into Janet in slow, precise blows.

Silence filled the room as Janet attempted to recover from Emily's verbal assault. The girl had laid there so quiet for so long that she never expected this from her. She felt her own anger rise and had no intention of pushing it back down.

Janet's eyes narrowed and before Emily knew what was happening, she felt the sting of a hard slap across her face. Her eyes watered and her own hand flew to her cheek, which now felt hot and swollen. She could tell her mouth was hanging open in shock. Janet's violent act did nothing to squelch Emily's anger. Were she mobile, she would have been on top of the woman in a second, beating the pulp out of her.

"I haven't taken you captive. You should be grateful that I found you and rescued you." Janet's height had risen in defiance and she now stood rigid, looking down at Emily. When she had ordered a girl from the service, she hoped the girl would be so overjoyed at Janet rescuing her that she might want to stay indefinitely.

But this girl was never going to love Janet. She was a reject. Janet wanted to demand another, but she doubted that the service would take her back. And what were they to do with her anyway, kill her?

"You aren't going anywhere. This is your new home and you should get used to it. Your ankle will heal. They always do. There is no escape for you here, so you better spend your time getting acclimated to your new surroundings."

Expending anger had felt good to Emily initially, but now she could see how it had backfired. With Janet angry, she would have an even harder time. She had no idea where or how far away from home she was. The one thing she did know was that her parents would not stop looking for her.

Carrie had slipped out of Bracket's office and later she watched as Randy walked back to their desks. His face was set with a fixed smile that encompassed the entire bottom of his face. His eyes twinkled with joy and the anticipation of fatherhood.

"Congratulations," Carrie said. She was genuinely happy for Randy, but it was a reminder that she had been on the same track to get married and have a family when she had blown it all up. Randy's wonderful news shed an enormous spotlight on Carrie's emotional disfunction. The moment was bittersweet, but not something she was willing to rectify.

Randy stopped at his desk and looked at Carrie. "Thank you." He had grown to know Carrie pretty well the past two years. When her engagement had faltered and she and Billy had broken it off, Randy had felt genuinely sad for her. He also didn't know how to help with the growing emotional disassociation he saw happening within her.

Carrie coughed and looked away. "So, while you were in there with Bracket, I called the Human Trafficking Task Force head, Andrew Gulch. I thought that since we highly suspect that these girls are being taken because of a trafficking ring, then they might be able to point us in the right direction or share some leads."

Randy was nodding his head, deep in thought. "Good. So, what did he say?"

"Well, he was more than willing to help in any way that he could. He had the files on the girls and had added them to their growing list of missing women and children. But he said their primary focus was not on the individuals that had gone missing, but on the overall trafficking organization. They were spending their time on leads to arrest and charge those involved and running the game, and then hopefully finding many of the abductees.

"To focus on one abducted person at a time slowed them down

since it would take their focus off the overall big picture. But he said he will share everything they have with us. Then he asked how confident we were that someone had abducted them because of human trafficking."

"How can we be sure at this point?" Randy asked as much to himself as to Carrie.

Carrie could see Randy was running their two cases through his mind, comparing them to what he knew about human trafficking. "The truth is, we have two missing girls and nothing to tie them together. We honestly don't even know if the same unsub took them."

Randy flopped down in his chair, the huge smile tucked away for another time.

"What do we do now?" Carrie asked.

Randy looked up as his mental wheels were attempting to gain traction. "Let's go retrace what we've done so far." He got up and started towards the room they had dedicated to these cases. The white board stood waiting and ready to receive more clues.

Randy popped the lid off of a marker. He wrote young Alex's name under Emily's and made a note of pertinent information that they had received from Alex. "We know pretty much what he looks like. We know he has the NT initial tattoo. We know the car he was driving, the blue 2002 Honda Civic."

"Did the tattoo appear to be professionally done or one done himself?" Carrie asked.

"Or in prison." Randy added.

He pulled a close-up of the tattoo from their file and held it up where they could both see it. "The lines are incredibly straight." Randy noticed.

"The proportions are pretty tight, too. The N and the T are both very balanced as if designed that way."

"If someone did it in prison or did it at home, I can't see it being that refined," Randy said.

He tacked the picture up on the whiteboard. "So let's say it was a tattoo parlor tattoo. There are dozens in the OKC and surrounding areas." He looked at Carrie, searching her face.

"All I know to do is start calling. We could drive around all day going from one to another, but we will cover more on the phone." Carrie didn't look forward to more phone time, but she looked forward to catching hold of another lead.

"I worked this morning while you were gone on the list of car owners. I only got partway through. Would you like to work on that while I call tattoo artists?" Carrie thought at least it would be more interesting than finding the owner of the car.

"Sure. Switch it up a bit." Randy looked back at the board. "I don't want this case to grow cold. I don't want to go tell these parents that their daughters are gone and may never be coming home."

Chapter Fifteen

The man had watched the girl. He had seen her walk to her home and now he knew where she lived. The organization had sent him a message already, impatient for a red-headed girl. He had only seen her leave in a car and then once in her front yard getting the mail.

He would be a fool to try to take her from her own front yard, but then...

The roast beef in his Philly sub was more interesting at the moment than the girl. He hadn't eaten all day and felt like he was starving. At the first bite, the sensational flavor awakened his taste buds and his stomach begged to receive the goods.

He shut his eyes in ecstasy. This was his favorite meal, and he intended to savor every bite.

Deep into his food high, he heard metal clanking and a soft motor whirring. He looked up at the house, expecting a car to back out of the garage. Nothing emerged for a beat or two, then out came the red-headed girl on a bicycle.

She zipped down the driveway and turned down the street in the opposite direction of the man and his sub.

What shitty timing. He turned the key with one hand and held his sub in the other. He would eat and drive.

The girl peddled through several of the tree-lined neighborhood streets. By all appearances, this was a safe, cozy and family-friendly neighborhood. The man huffed at the thought. *If they only knew.*

After about six or seven turns, the girl pulled into another driveway and stopped, leaning her bike against a short railing on the front porch. She stood ringing the bell until another girl answered and led her inside.

Good. That would give him time to eat. He would snatch her on her ride home.

~

Peggy's revelation that she needed to give Melinda back was fraught with complications. She paced the floor, thinking. *How can I give her back and not get caught? I can't get caught.*

Melinda watched and waited. She could see Peggy's struggle. From the little bit of mumbling that she could make out, she was trying to figure a way to get Melinda home and get away with what she had done.

Melinda didn't care. She saw Peggy as a broken, hurting woman who was lonely and just wanted someone to love. Melinda didn't think putting her away in prison would be the compassionate thing to do.

"Peggy, I know you may not believe me, but I don't want you to get caught. I don't want you to be arrested and go to jail." Melinda stopped at that to see if it would sink in, and how Peggy would respond.

She stopped her pacing and turned and looked at the girl. Her hands were wringing in front of her. Her pained expression focused on Melinda.

"I know you say that, but once you are away from here, you will tell. You will have no reason not to. I don't know what to do." Peggy flopped down into the overstuffed chair facing Melinda and dropped her head into her hands.

Knowing this was a tricky situation, Melinda sat trying to think of what the correct response would be. Peggy could change her mind at any second and decide she would not give Melinda back. The realization that the woman had intended to keep her permanently played tug-of-war with Melinda's emotions. From compassion for her, to anger at the thought she had intended to keep Melinda permanently.

"I can just leave. You don't have to take me anywhere. In fact, once I leave, you can too. You can go away somewhere else where they will never find you. But, I promise you Peggy. I won't give you away."

Melinda felt time slow to a crawl as she waited. Finally, Peggy decided, "I have to think more about it. You can stay just a while longer until I decide, can't you? You'll be okay with that, won't you?" she asked with pleading eyes.

Melinda gave the poor, pathetic woman a soft smile and nodded.

~

The drudgery of making phone calls was wearing thin on both Randy and Carrie. Keeping her mind focused on the repetitive response from each and every tattoo artist caused Carrie to lose focus, so she barely heard… "I did do that tattoo. He was a cool guy." It took Carrie a second to realize what the lady had just said. She bolted upright in her chair, suddenly hyper-focused.

"What can you tell me about him?"

"Well, I'm not sure. It was a quick tat, so he wasn't here long."

"How long ago was this?" Carrie asked.

"Mmm, I guess about a month ago." Hope lifted Carrie's spirits. With such little time gone by, the odds of the artist remembering more was probable.

"You don't happen to have any security video still on hand, do you?" Carrie held her breath.

"Naw, I don't have any of that right now. I've talked about it, but I'm just getting started and money is tight." The air left Carrie in a rush.

"Okay. Okay. That's fine. Do you think you could draw us a picture of the man, or come in and work with our sketch artist? All we have is a grainy still frame from a video. We need a really good sketch to show around."

"Yeah, I could do that for you. I took art in college. People say I'm really good." Carrie smiled.

"You would be such a help to us. When do you think you could do it?"

"I'm not busy now."

"Okay, we can come down. We need to take an official statement and we will pick up the drawing. You have been more help than you can imagine. Thank you so much!"

Randy was on the phone when Carrie hung up. One hand holding the receiver and the other rested on his forehead. He was as tired of making calls as she was.

Carrie wanted to interrupt, but just stood by, tense and ready. The second he pulled the phone away from his ear, she blurted, "I've got something."

"You do? What?"

"I found the tattoo artist who did the tattoo. She is going to draw us a pic of the man. He got the tattoo a month ago, and she remembered him. I told her we would come down and talk with her and take an official statement. She's going to start on the drawing right now."

Getting the first genuine lead since speaking with Alex buoyed their energy, and they were soon out the door.

The tattoo parlor was close to the Paseo district, a vibrant and fun artist's paradise. It took a few runs through the surrounding area to actually find the tiny building. It had once been the detached garage of a refurbished house that sat just one block off of Paseo Drive. The house was now an art gallery and had drawn their attention away from the tiny tattoo parlor to the side in the back.

There were no other cars in the drive, but Randy still pulled alongside the curb out front. It was a nice day, and the large mature trees cast a soothing shade.

A bell tinkled as the door swung open. A girl who appeared to be in her mid twenties stood behind a small counter. She had displayed tattoo options and photos of completed tattoos on the walls.

"Are you Ava?" Randy asked, displaying his wallet badge.

"Yes. Are you the agents who wanted me to draw a pic of the guy?"

"We are," said Carrie.

Ava came from behind the counter with a pencil drawing of the man. They could tell it was the same man in the grainy video still. Ava had done an amazing job.

"Ava, this is great." Carrie was elated.

"Is there a place where we can sit down? We would like to ask you a few questions," said Randy.

Ava spun this way and that, surveying their small surroundings. "I have a small table outside we can go sit at."

Randy smiled at the freshness and innocence of Ava. One would miss it at first glance with her black attire, wild hair, and various piercings. "That will work fine."

The trio sat crowded around a tiny table on the shop's back porch. There was shade and a subtle breeze that cooled the air.

Randy pulled out his small notepad and pen. "Can you tell us what the man's name is?"

Ava frowned a bit. "Joe. Joseph I think."

"Do you know his last name?"

She said with her face in stern reflection. "I'm not sure. He paid in cash, so I didn't run a card."

"Okay. That's fine. Was he just a walk-in customer or did someone refer him?"

"Oh, a friend referred him. Actually, I am so new that to get a referral is wonderful."

"And who was it that referred him?" Both Carrie and Randy were half holding their breath. They needed something. This couldn't be another dead end.

"Uh," Ava hesitated.

Randy was patient as they waited for Ava.

"Bruno Sanchez. He was my very first customer." Ava beamed.

"Do you have contact info for Mr. Sanchez?"

Ava's smile faltered. "I'm not sure I'm supposed to give that to you. Isn't that a bad thing for a businessperson to do? Give out their clients' information?"

They didn't want to lie to Ava, but they wanted it. "We can go to a judge and get a warrant to get the info, but I don't think you would want us to have to do that, do you?"

She sat and thought a minute, struggling with making the right decision. "Can I call him and tell him and see if it is okay with him? I don't want to make him mad at me. He might not come back."

"And if he says no, then we will still get it with a warrant. We understand you have a new business you are trying to make a go of, but we are trying to find leads that will help us find two girls that have been abducted." Carrie said.

Ava took a deep breath and said, "Okay. Let me go get it for you." She left them at the table, breathing a collective sigh of relief.

"I feel like we are slowly getting somewhere. I just hope the girls can survive while we slog through all of this to get to them." Carrie said.

Chapter Sixteen

It was just turning from dusk to evening when the girl finally left to head for home. She was focused on disengaging her bike from the porch rail and turning to face home.

The man started his car and headed quietly down the street in the direction he knew she would travel back home. Seeing a particularly dense grove of trees and bushes, he pulled over just beyond, and sat watching for the girl.

He got out and was sitting in his front passenger seat with the door slightly ajar. He was ready to pounce the second he saw her, and knew she was close enough to grab as she traveled down the sidewalk.

As she turned the corner, Olivia saw the blue Honda sitting next to the curb, but there was nothing about it that alarmed her. The landscaping in front of her was protruding out into the sidewalk and she mentally adjusted her route to accommodate. Just before getting to the blue Honda, she twisted her handlebars and jutted out from the sidewalk and into the street to go around the car.

Her abrupt action disoriented the man. That wasn't what he

had expected her to do, and now he was not positioned where he could grab her quickly and quietly.

He pulled the passenger door fully closed and attempted to slide back to the driver's side of the car as best he could with the gear shifter in the way. By the time he could start the car, the girl had whizzed past him and was a block and a half away. He cursed, started the car, and sped away from the curb. Now he was forced to react without a solid plan. That was never good.

One block from her home, he nosed his car past her and suddenly cut in front of her, forcing her to apply her brakes. He jumped out of the car, ran around to the passenger side and grabbed her off of the bike.

As he was struggling to open the car door, she began screaming at the top of her lungs. He released the door handle and placed that hand over her mouth, the other hand gripping her around her middle. She was kicking and pummeling him with her elbows.

Lights were flipping on in the surrounding houses, so he dropped to the ground while still holding the girl in an effort to hide the best that he could. His mind raced trying to decide the best course of action. He needed a redhead girl and once he had found this one; he had had to wait far too long to take her. This opportunity might not come along again quickly.

She continued to struggle against the man, but being caught in the squat of his body reduced her mobility. His hand tightened further around her mouth and his nails pinched into her face. He could feel her tears running over his fingers.

His other arm formed a steel vice around her upper body and he continued to squeeze from sheer panic. Frustration continued to build as he attempted to decide what to do. He was a powder keg ready to blow. High blood pressure caused a roar through his ears and it pressed against the top of his skull. He cursed himself for his lack of patience. He knew he should have never tried to improvise.

"Stop fighting me," came a low and guttural growl into her ear. The sheer power of the delivery of those words caused the opposite effect, and Olivia struggled even harder. She bit the inside of the man's hand and tasted the metallic blood in her mouth.

Fury burst through the man and in one swift movement, he let go and grabbed her around the neck, forcing her down to the ground. He pushed forcibly on her neck, his rage causing his senses to wane and his eyes to bulge. He would make sure she quit fighting him. There was no thought of consequences or repercussions. Beyond furious, he just pushed and pushed.

When his senses once again surfaced and seeped into the anger, pushing his animalistic response aside, he looked at the unmoving girl. Her bright green eyes were open and round in shock. Her mouth was slightly open. She was dead.

He jerked his hand from her neck and scurried backwards. Stunned at what he had done, he quickly assessed his surroundings. The neighborhood had grown quiet again with the subsiding screams. He duck-walked around to his driver's side door. Slipping in behind the wheel and driving away, he left Olivia and her bicycle on the dark neighborhood street.

Emily could tell that she was running a fever. She shivered and couldn't get warm. In the hot tin trailer on a summer day, that should have been impossible. *Broken bones don't cause a fever or infection, do they?*

She moved the quilt Janet had given her. It hurt as it brushed her swollen foot. When it finally fell away, Emily gasped at the sight of her foot. It bulged even further around the bandage and there were violent red streaks shooting up her leg.

"Oh God," cried Emily. "My foot! My foot! Take me to the

hospital!" She burst out bawling. She knew if she wasn't tended to, she might lose her foot, her leg, or her life.

Janet silently walked back into the room and looked down at Emily. The foot looked bad. She had done her best to clean the scrapes and the puncture from the tree root, but she was not a nurse and now realized that she had not done enough to ward off infection.

Janet sank into a chair opposite of the sofa where Emily lay. As she stared through the dingy shag carpeting that covered the living room floor, the realization that she could not keep the girl surfaced and took hold. She couldn't just let her die either, could she? No one knew she was there. She could let her die and then dispose of her in the woods. She could put her back in the box and seal the lid and cover it with earth, leaves, and twigs. No one would ever find her.

Emily's screams pierced Janet's attempts to decide what to do. "Take me to the hospital!"

This girl had been nothing but trouble from the very beginning. She would demand her money back. Or a replacement. No, this had been enough for her. She would not try again.

As Janet sat crumpled in the chair, sadness crept into her soul as she realized she couldn't buy love. She couldn't force someone to love her. Nothing she would do would be good enough for this girl, or for anyone else, to ever love her.

Janet sat nearly catatonic, staring into space for over thirty minutes, as all hope dissipated from her. Her body shut out the girl's screams and nothing existed but the black hole of despair she had fallen into. Finally, she woodenly stood up from the chair and walked down the hallway to the back bedroom of the house.

Emily stopped screaming and watched as Janet walked away. *Is she going to help me*? A small bit of hope surfaced. Then in the silence she heard the gunshot ring out through the old trailer.

Emily's mouth hung open in shock. The thought that her

captor had done the unimaginable just couldn't be true. Emily continued to sit up on one elbow, looking down the hallway, waiting for Janet to say something or to emerge from the room.

Panic surged through her brain so fiercely that it felt as though her head would explode. Emily screamed for Janet for what seemed like hours, but no response ever came. Her vision became disoriented and unfocused. She felt her body flush first with a searing hot wave, then with frigid cold. The shock exhausted her further, and she lay back down on the sofa.

When Janet had killed herself, Emily knew that she had killed her too.

~

Carrie's phone jolted her from sleep. It was her night for abstinence, which to her was the six-pack and pizza instead of a half a fifth of Jack Daniels. She had fallen asleep early on her sofa. She looked through blurry eyes and reached for the phone on her coffee table.

"Carrie Border," she croaked out.

"You okay?" Randy asked.

Carrie coughed to clear her throat and sat up straight. "Yeah. I just fell asleep on the sofa and the phone woke me up." Her voice was still hoarse. She sat, rubbing her face with her free hand as her senses came back to life.

"We have been called in by Matt Booker. They have a dead girl. When he got to the scene, he felt it was a failed attempt to take another girl, and he asked us to meet him at the scene."

Carrie was instantly alert. "Send me the address." Realizing it wasn't far from her home, she said, "Be there in ten."

The neighborhood was lit with flashing red and blue lights. Carrie had to park nearly a block away. She flashed her wallet badge to the various guardians who were protecting the scene from onlookers. She took in her surroundings as she walked to the epicenter of the activity.

Matt Booker stood beside a girl's body. The coroner, Henry Bloom, was squatting beside her and looked up as Carrie approached.

The large swath of purple across the young girl's throat was a clear indicator of strangulation. *But, is it the primary cause of death?*

"COD?" she asked

Henry stood and faced Carrie. "From my preliminary exam, I would say strangulation. Quite violently, too. But when I get her back to the morgue, I may determine it was something else."

Pain from gut-piercing screams, sliced through Carrie's heart. She closed her eyes as she heard the young girl's mother. She knew officers were compassionately holding her back from seeing her daughter in such a state, and Carrie vowed to do whatever she could to catch this man.

Chapter Seventeen

Peggy had spent more time pacing the floor than enjoying Melinda's company. It had all gone so wrong.

She couldn't force someone to love her, regardless of manipulation through love or harm. Love had to be freely given, or it wasn't love at all. As this reality settled within Peggy's heart, she became even more distraught.

Peggy had spent her life on this farm. She had very little income, but since the farm had no debt, there were few expenses. If she left the farm, she would have to get another job besides selling the few crocheted items she sat in her home and made. Her entire world would change.

How could she leave the home she had grown up in, even though the memories of her childhood had tainted her entire life while living here? Now that she realized just how much her parents had loved her, even though their ability to show it had been handicapped, she felt differently about her home here on the farm.

She paced back and forth, caught in her own personal vortex of tumultuous thoughts and attempts at trying to decide.

Melinda had done little through the day, attempting to stay out of Peggy's way so she would hopefully come to the right conclusion. She had gone to sleep in the frilly bed and had slept surprisingly well.

Thoughts of attempting to escape kept surfacing, but she pushed them down, hoping that Peggy would finally decide to free her. If that happened, then she could return home without the possibility of harm coming to either of them.

A failed attempt at escaping could turn the tide and make Peggy change her mind and heart about letting Melinda go. So, she had played the game yet one more day.

By eight a.m. in the morning, the house was filled with the scent of bacon frying. Melinda followed the sizzling sounds to the kitchen. She was so hungry. Dinner the previous evening had been a sandwich. It was fine then, but hadn't lasted through the night.

The sight before Melinda as she turned the corner and came through the kitchen doorway was an array of breakfast foods. An enormous platter of pancakes stood next to a pile of crisp bacon strips. Peggy was removing the last strips from the frying pan and placing them on the pile. Melinda watched as the woman poured a prepared bowl of scrambled eggs into the bacon grease.

Toast popped up out of the toaster and Peggy hurried to retrieve it, quickly releasing it onto yet another plate. She shook her fingers and blew on them, feeling the burn from the hot toast. She was in such a focused state that Melinda didn't dare disturb her. As she watched the effort that the woman was putting into such an enormous meal, her heart broke for Peggy.

"Wow, are we having company for breakfast?" asked Melinda. She smiled warmly at Peggy. "It all looks so good and I'm hungry, too."

Peggy turned around, surprised to see Melinda standing there. A warm smile filled her face. She loved the girl, whether she should or not. "Can you get the silverware?" Peggy pointed to a drawer close by Melinda.

"Sure. Only for us?" Melinda once again probed.

"Yes, only us," Peggy blushed at her over-productive array of breakfast food. She knew it was too much, but she had just dove in enthusiastically earlier that morning and couldn't stop herself.

Melinda helped Peggy move the bounty to the kitchen table, once again decorated with a frilly table runner and two placemats. With their plates, cloth napkins, utensils, and the platters of food, there was barely room for the added small vase of fresh flowers.

Peggy heaped one type of food after another onto Melinda's plate and the girl eagerly dove in and ate as though she hadn't eaten in years.

As she ate, she watched Melinda enjoy breakfast. It brought her far more comfort than satiating her own hunger. It thrilled Peggy to see her eat so heartily and with such joy. It dawned on her that she had truly come to love the girl in the short time they had been together. She also realized that love demanded she be returned to her true family. The bittersweetness snuffed Peggy's hunger, and she laid her fork down.

"We aren't in Nebraska," said Peggy as she watched Melinda clean the last bite from her plate.

"I'm done," the man yelled into the phone. "I'm out. No more."

Silence echoed through the phone. The silence from the other end was more chilling than any words could have ever been.

A ripple of fear ran down the man's spine, followed by anger bringing him to his senses. "Something went wrong last night and now that girl is dead. I'm out." The last words trailing off into a soft wish. He knew that if they didn't want him out, he wouldn't be. In fact, just saying it was a death wish.

The line went dead without a word being uttered. Nausea bent the man in two. His ears began ringing, and he felt dizzy.

Forcing himself to push past his physical fear, he knew he had to get out of the house and away as soon as possible. He rose and flew into his bedroom, grabbing a large duffle bag and shoving clothes into it as quickly as possible. A minute later, he stood in the center of his small house and looked around. *Is there anything else I will definitely need?*

Finally, he shook his head and headed for the door.

He stopped just off of I-40, somewhere past the town of Shawnee for gas, a good 40 miles from home. The station was old and small and looked to be used only by the locals. He was still avoiding being seen if he could. He felt some relief as he left Midwest City, the eastern metropolitan edge of the Oklahoma City area. His mind was now planning where he would actually go and what he would do.

His last thought before the knife plunged deep into his back and up through his heart was that he had done it. He was free.

Carrie and Randy had assisted the OKCPD patrol officers and Detective Booker in canvasing the houses in the area. Carrie wanted to act immediately on any actionable information as soon as they got it, and being here in the field would give her a step up.

"Yes, I heard her screams." The woman they were talking with lived in the house in front of where Olivia had been killed. The woman was distraught. "I looked out, but didn't see anything. I guess the hedge in my front yard was too tall to see. The screams stopped, and I finally stopped looking."

"Did you see a car?" Carrie asked.

The woman thought for only a second before answering. "Yes.

There was a blue, I think, car. An import, not sure what kind. It was just turning dark out."

"Maybe one like this?" Carrie held out a picture of the blue Honda Civic they had pulled from the video surveillance and then one they had printed off of the internet.

The woman studied the picture and nodded. "Yes, I think that is it. It was just too dark and then with the large rose hedge." The woman's head shook slightly as her words drifted off.

Randy stopped writing notes on his notepad and pulled out the picture of the man they had obtained in surveillance. "Does this man look remotely familiar? Have you seen him around here at all?" He gave her a few moments to think, then pulled out the sketches that Alex had helped with and the one that Ava had done. They were nearly identical. "These sketches may be better."

The agents could tell she wanted to tell them yes, that she had seen him. They could see how badly she wanted to help. She looked up at them with sadness weighing on her face. "No. I'm sorry. I haven't seen him." Her apologetic voice was nearly a whisper.

Chapter Eighteen

Melinda just stared at Peggy. Then, as the realization of her words sunk in, her eyes narrowed and she asked, "What do you mean we are not in Nebraska?" Her tone came across as measured and controlled. She didn't know why it surprised her that Peggy had lied about where they were.

Peggy had crossed a line she knew she could not return from. She had launched into the truth and she knew she must now finish it. She looked down at her hands in her lap, ashamed of what she had done.

Melinda let the question hover in the air. Then again, with quieter force, "What do you mean we are not in Nebraska? Where are we?"

Peggy slowly lifted her face to look at Melinda. "We are east of Oklahoma City."

It was another shockwave that hit Melinda. The realization that they were so close to her home brought relief coupled with intense anger. Two emotions fought to take control and in the fight, Melinda had no words to express what she was feeling.

Peggy could see the rage on Melinda's face as the girl stood, eyes fixed on her the entire time. "I'm leaving."

Melinda knew that if she was this close to Oklahoma City, then she could start walking in any direction and would soon come to a small town or other houses. Her chair scraped loudly against the hard linoleum floor and she turned away from the beautifully laid out kitchen table and tearful woman.

She walked to the front door, opened it, and looked out. It was a beautiful day with the birds chirping and the sun shining. Melinda shut her eyes and took a deep breath as a broad smile washed across her face. She was going home.

"Forensics found touch DNA on Olivia's skin. We have a match in the DNA database and found him in CODIS. We know his name." Randy was rapidly giving Carrie the news. Finally, they had something. Finally, it felt like they had traction in the case.

"Did you run him to see what kind of car he drives?" Carrie asked, her fingers already poised over her keyboard.

"No, here you go." Randy handed her the file.

Carrie typed as fast as she could and hoped for a match. The computer labored, then flashed the results on the screen. Her eyes scanned and when she saw what she had hoped was there, she let out a cry of joy. "It's him."

They followed through with a statewide APB on the man and his car. His known work history showed he was employed at a local grocery store. They had both his home and work address and were quickly out the door.

"I want to feel relieved, and I do, but what if this is a bust?" Carrie asked.

"A bust?" Randy looked over at Carrie. "Won't be," he said, determined, and looked back at the road.

"I don't know. I've got a funny feeling about this, and I want to find those girls as soon as possible, and alive, not dead. But something doesn't feel right in my gut."

"Do you think he might just be Olivia's killer and not the kidnapper?" Randy was trying to figure out why Carrie felt off about the new lead.

"I can't put my finger on it. I think he is the one. He matches Alex's description, car and everything. It's just a feeling that something isn't quite right."

The man, Joseph Savage, they now knew, lived in a suburb of Oklahoma City called Warr Acres. It was close to Emily and Melinda, but Olivia had lived a few miles away. They were soon pulling into the driveway of a small white frame house across the street from a high school. There was no car in the driveway.

As Carrie stepped out of the car, she turned and looked at the high school. "Well, talk about a fox in the henhouse."

Randy turned to look at the large brick building that had grown quiet for the summer. "Yes, except the girls who have gone missing are all middle school age, and he doesn't have any sexual offenses on his record. There was no way to know or to keep him away from the school."

They were careful to close their doors softly, aware that the sound could alert him of their arrival, if he didn't already know. They approached the house on high alert. Carrie, with one hand on her sidearm.

Randy knocked loudly on the front screen door, which rattled violently. "OSBI agents. Open up." Randy had pulled his weapon and was ready should the unexpected happen.

When he heard no sound, he opened the screen door and knocked even harder on the front wooden door, giving the same instruction. Still no answer.

"He's not home. His car is gone. Do we have our warrant yet?"

Randy stepped back from the door and looked at his phone.

"Yes, we do." As he spoke, two OKCPD patrol cars pulled in along the curb and the officers got out.

There were quick greetings. The small group stood by as Randy tried the doorknob. It was locked, so he kicked at the rickety door, which burst open with little effort.

The forensic team arrived and waited for the all clear. The tiny house was easy to search and soon all present were in and looking for clues. They dusted a desktop computer for prints. Since it was password protected, it was bagged and taken away. After two hours of searching hard, Randy and Carrie left it to the team and headed back to the office.

"There was no sign of the girls in there." Randy was tired and ready to go home.

Carrie sat quietly, sorting through her thoughts one thread at a time. "What are the odds he is not our guy?"

Randy rubbed his eyes. "He has to be. You still have that feeling?" He glanced over at Carrie.

"I do. Something isn't right."

"We'll see if the team turns up anything and we'll start fresh in the morning. When we get back, we can update Matt and check with the task force to see if they have had any dealings with a Joseph Savage."

Void of the earlier adrenaline, Carrie and Randy shuffled into the office and flopped into their seats. Neither one said anything for the next half hour as they composed reports and notified the necessary personnel.

As Carrie was working her way through her email, one caught her attention. "Randy."

"Yep."

Carrie looked at Randy with her mouth hanging open. "He's dead."

Frowning, Randy replied, "What do you mean, he's dead?"

"They found him and his car at a gas station east of Shawnee along I-40. He was laying out by the gas pumps, dead. He was stabbed in the back."

Carrie didn't know if it was bar night or abstinence night, but she honestly couldn't care less. She was going to drink herself senseless. She had known something wasn't right in her gut, but had no idea what it was or what to do about it.

Joseph Savage had been their only lead to the girls and now he was gone and the girls were still out there. The thought that there was someone much higher up in the chain pulling the strings was now a very good probability. Killing Olivia seemed like a screwup, and he had paid the price. He had known it and was running for his life.

The regular crowd was there, in their usual places. Wade gave her a smile and turned to grab her usual. "Hey Wade. How's it going?" Carrie asked as she slid onto a bar stool.

He turned around and sat the amber bottle in front of her. "Looks like I should be asking you that. You, no offense, look like shit."

Carrie was quickly downing the beer. As she put it back on the bar with a loud thunk, she responded, "I feel like shit. It was a horribly hard day at work."

"Well, I know you can't say much, but if you ever want to talk, I'm here." For the first time, she looked at Wade, really looked at him. He was undoubtedly handsome with his wavy blonde hair. He was fit, but not in an obvious way. For an instant, she thought about lowering the drawbridge to her soul, but then just as quickly changed her mind.

"Thank you Wade." Her thanks were heartfelt and she could tell Wade knew. "It is hard talking about myself. My job, my personal life, anything really."

"I get it. Still, if you need to or if you want to, I'm here."

Carrie tipped the bottle and swallowed the last of the beer. "Thanks for the drink but, I am going to need something a little stronger tonight." Wade raised a questioning eyebrow. "Jack and Coke on the rocks. Make it a double."

"You got it," Wade replied and soon Carrie had left memories of the job, the girls, and the dead killer behind.

Chapter Nineteen

Melinda had been walking for what seemed like forever. The path in front of Peggy's house was a dirt road of hard-packed and rutted red clay. What began as a near run soon turned into a slow walk. The road was hard to walk on, and Melinda had nearly tripped over the ruts more than once.

The beautiful sunny day was now nearing triple digits, and she was baking. Between slapping the mosquitos and other flying insects, and wiping away the sweat that dripped in her eyes, Melinda was miserable.

She had sincerely thought that by now she would have come upon another house or small town. Peggy may have lied about being in Nebraska, but she hadn't been lying when she said they were a long way from town.

Peggy hadn't followed her. She had thought that she might and was watching over her shoulder for the first half mile or so, but she never came. She felt bad for the lonely old woman who had clearly never really known what love was. But Melinda wasn't the person to show her.

Melinda knew she needed to stop for a break. She stepped over to the side of the road, found a tree with some decent shade, and made a place in the weeds underneath to sit. Propping her arms on her bent knees, she wondered where she really was. She wasn't familiar with her surroundings. There were woods and a few pastures, and there had been one field of something she didn't recognize.

Her feet ached, and she itched. She looked down at her feet, debating whether or not to rest by taking off her shoes. They both hurt, but her right foot particularly throbbed. She slid her shoe off of her heel just slightly and sure enough, there was a huge burst blister. "Dang."

She left her foot in the shoe and bent the back down to rest under her heel. This would slow her down, but she knew if she kept walking, she would eventually find someone. The bark of the tree was hard as she laid her head back, but it felt good to rest. Soon she was fast asleep.

~

Carrie woke up laying next to Wade, but she wasn't in her own bed. When she opened her eyes, the room spun, and the bed did somersaults. She held her forehead with her hand and hoped she could gain enough composure to get up. The night before was a blur, and after her third Jack and Coke, she didn't remember a thing.

"What a lightweight," she mumbled to herself.

"Lightweight?" Wade said, rolling over to look at her. "Do you have any idea how much you drank last night?"

"No."

"I cut you off and you about took my head off, but luckily you were so drunk that I could man-handle you. I put you in the back, in my office, and you passed out on the sofa. Later, I woke you up enough to get you into my car." Wade watched her lay there stone still. Finally, she dropped her hand from her forehead and turned her face to him.

Carrie opened her mouth to say something, but the words wouldn't come. A few moments later, she opened her mouth again to speak. When nothing came out for the second time, she shut her eyes and turned to look at the ceiling.

"Carrie, I don't know you well, but the little I have gotten to know you, I admire. You are a wonderful vibrant woman with so much to offer." Carrie snorted, but let him continue. "The work you do is so critical and I can tell you do it well because you care.

"If you continue down this road, you will hit a brick wall. At the least, it could render you useless in law enforcement, at the most it could kill you. Either way, the world would suffer a tremendous loss, and I would miss you."

Carrie continued to lie quietly. Random tears found their way from the corners of her eyes to the pillow beneath her.

"I don't know what has caused you so much pain and self loathing, but I can say that it is unjustified." Wade stopped. He had said all he needed to say.

He reached over and took one of her hands and entwined his fingers with hers. "I am always here for you if and when you need to talk, or even when you don't."

Those words popped pin holes in her emotional bubble and she allowed herself to cry softly. She rolled over to Wade and allowed him to hold her. She knew she couldn't have it both ways, walled off emotionally from pain, or caring for others without getting hurt herself. The two didn't intermingle. But for now, for this moment, she needed to be held.

It was supposed to be Carrie's day off, but she was restless and went to the office, anyway. She had fallen back asleep in Wade's arms and slept for another hour, allowing her headache to subside and her body to recover. She vowed to be more in control and not drink so much, but in the same internal breath, she knew she needed the drink to dull the pain she refused to feel.

The office was quiet. There was only a skeleton group of agents in on the weekends. They rotated on-call unless they were working an urgent case. Carrie felt her case was just that - urgent. She also knew that Randy needed family time, so she was fine working in the quiet of the office alone.

As soon as she logged into her computer, she reviewed any additional notes or reports that had been submitted. There were still no updates from forensics on Olivia. They had gotten the DNA from the man and that had led them to find him. Were he still alive, that would have led to his conviction.

But Carrie knew that someone else had orchestrated this entire ordeal. Could they find the thread that lead upwards and convict him as an accessory to her murder? Had Joseph not been told to take her, she would not be dead. Thin and thready at best. She would put that thought aside for now.

Her primary concern was the two missing girls, Emily and Melinda. *Are they still alive, and are they even in Oklahoma or have they been taken to another state or country?*

She saw a message in her email inbox from Matt Booker. He had no additional news to report, either. Another email from Andrew Gulch at the human trafficking task force was there as well.

They had never heard of Joseph Savage and, as far as they knew, he had no ties to their known circle of human trafficking thugs. But of course, he continued, there are always new recruits coming aboard the ship of evil.

Carrie sat back in her chair, tapping her bottom lip with her finger. She had to clear and separate the things they knew from the things they suspected.

They knew Joseph Savage had killed Olivia. They knew he had also taken Emily. That concretely tied him to both girls. They did not know for certain that he had taken Melinda, so she pushed that to the side for a bit.

They knew he had been killed right after word got around about Olivia's murder. They still couldn't definitely say that his murder tied him to Olivia's death, even though she knew in her heart it was true. She pushed that over into the unknown category.

With so little known facts, it tempted her to feel lost. Her mind took her back to the day she had looked for older cases with the same M.O. She had nearly gotten through it, but Randy had interrupted her when it had come time to interview Alex with his parents. She needed to finish that. And what if it were statewide?

She popped her chair forward and began typing furiously, hyper-focused on the task at hand. It took another hour to finish going through open and cold cases of missing or dead girls in the age range of 11 to 14.

There were no open cases for the last ten years for murdered girls that age in Oklahoma. *Kudos to us*. They had solved all of those and none matched the details they were facing with the current case.

She perused the files of the few remaining missing girls. They were a possibility. She made notes to herself and retrieved the files of those she thought were the most likely.

She stood and stretched. The day had crept into the late afternoon and she hadn't eaten all day. Maybe she would save contacting the local FBI to see about broadening her search until Monday.

Carrie logged out of her computer and tidied her desk before leaving. In doing so, she uncovered a two-inch square sticky note that had gotten stuck to the underneath side of a file.

Someone had taken the note late the day before and it read; *Woman has info on the missing girl named Melinda. Her name is Peggy Bishop* and a contact phone was listed. Carrie couldn't believe her eyes. Was she really seeing the note correctly? All thoughts of hunger evacuated her body, and she felt physically rejuvenated.

She wouldn't bother Randy. It could be a loose rabbit trail. When she knew if it was actionable, she would contact him.

Chapter Twenty

Melinda slept in the tree's shade for a few hours. She hadn't realized how exhausted she was. Finally, she started back down the dirt road, making very slow time. She had bent both of the heels in on her shoes so they would not rub her blisters, but they were not made to function as slides and she struggled to hold them on. They hadn't fit well in the first place, so it had reduced her progress to however fast she could hobble in the makeshift shoes.

She had tried to navigate by the sun, making a few turns, first one way and then another. She believed she was surely winding herself towards Oklahoma City. But what if she was on the opposite side and was, in fact, walking away from where she intended to go? Could she believe Peggy that they were east of Oklahoma City and not west?

Overwhelming despair threatened to engulf her, but she continued to force it away with sheer mental determination. She knew that eventually she would find someone. She just had to keep going.

The sky was painted with another beautiful Oklahoma sunset,

but Melinda couldn't enjoy it. Seeing the vivid oranges and yellows signaled the impending darkness that would soon fall on her. She wondered if she should keep going or stop for the night. But where should she stop? There were only woods around her on all sides, and she cursed herself for deciding to make the various turns instead of going straight. *What if I have only been going in circles?*

Only one vehicle had passed her that day. It was what had actually woken her up from her nap. She had been sound asleep off of the side of the road, leaning on the tree deep in the shade. The pickup truck had gone speeding down the road before she even realized what had happened.

The huge red dirt cloud exploded behind the moving truck and engulfed Melinda. By the time she had stumbled from underneath the tree to the road, it hid the truck, which was rapidly moving away from view.

The night sounds filled the air with a symphony of sound. It echoed in Melinda's ears and was shockingly loud. Small bits of light from the fireflies flitted about her as she tried to continue. The woods loomed forebodingly on each side and convinced her she should keep walking. But where to?

She had less of an idea where she was than when she had started, but knowing the sun always sets in the west gave her a sense of direction. *Am I east of Oklahoma City, or west of it?* The terrain and light had convinced her many times to take first one turn and then another. The truth was that she could be anywhere, even back close to Peggy's house.

The clunk of old boards on metal resonated through her feet. She was on an old bridge. Reaching out her hands, she felt the rusty metal railing. She followed it to the end, where it dipped and sloped gradually into the ground at the end of the bridge.

Exhaustion decided for her. She would sit down and lean back on the angled metal railing. She wouldn't be on the road, so there wouldn't be any risk of anyone hitting her. But she also wouldn't be in the dark woods. Maybe this close to the road someone would see her propped up there asleep.

The phone rang and rang, and Carrie nervously paced, waiting for someone to pick up the line. When no one answered and no answering message came on, she hung up and immediately tried again.

Who doesn't have voicemail on their phones these days? The phone continued to ring endlessly. Frustrated, she hung up and decided to try to see if she could locate the phone in their database and just go find the owner.

After about ten minutes, she found the phone was a landline registered to a woman named Peggy Bishop. The woman lived near Welty, Oklahoma. Carrie had lived in Oklahoma her entire life and had never heard of such a town.

With a few clicks on Google, she found Welty was a town of 131 residents. But the map didn't really show a traditional town, just a lot of random rural houses deep in the woods and far apart.

It was just over an hour northeast of Oklahoma City, just off of I-44, then several miles south. Carrie sat back in her chair and visually absorbed the map. This lady literally lived out in the middle of nowhere in a heavily wooded area. How on earth did Melinda get so far away from Oklahoma City and why? It didn't fit the theory of a human trafficking ring who bought and sold people for sexual profit.

As Carrie sat and thought, she realized that they could have sold this girl to a single person. Someone, a man probably, had bought her because he was lonely and wanted a sexual female companion. Maybe Emily had been taken and sold for the same reason.

The woman's location was a rural route or county road address. It wasn't really that close to Welty, but it was even further away from any other civilized area. From the satellite map, she zoomed in as far possible and could barely make out what looked like a small house at the end of a long dirt road deep in the woods.

Carrie looked at her watch. It was after eight p.m. She was even hungrier now than before. Melinda's life was hanging in the balance, but this woman was only a witness. With Carrie unable to reach her, she still didn't know if she knew something actionable or not. And how did she know Melinda's name, Carrie wondered.

By the time she drove way out to Peggy's house, it would be very late at night. And what if the lady wasn't there? She hadn't answered her home phone, so it seemed silly for Carrie to drive so far, only to confirm that the lady was indeed not home.

But what if the lady is also in danger because she tried to get information to us? That may be why she isn't answering her phone. The man may have found out and now both she and Melinda are in danger.

As she thought of various scenarios, she struggled with what decision to make. She finally decided that she would come in very early the next day and get with Randy to go with her. *That makes more sense, right?*

Carrie took a picture of the woman's address with her phone so she could call Randy early in the morning and give him the details.

~

Carrie was sitting in the drive-thru of the closest fast-food restaurant to her office. She was so hungry that she didn't care what she ate as long as it filled her up. Her mind could not leave Melinda and this new information. She needed to still her hunger so she could think.

Retrieving her bag of food, she pulled out into the parking lot and sat under a streetlamp. The first bite of the burger was amazing. But every bite thereafter became more and more robotic as she continued to trace every scenario in her mind regarding what she could do for Melinda.

When she had downed the last bite, she looked at her watch again. It was nearly nine p.m. She looked up and out into the night. Balling up her wrapper and tossing it into the floor, she checked her gas gauge and put her car in gear. She was going to go find Peggy and Melinda.

As she drove toward I-44, the thought crossed her mind to call Randy, but she did not want to disturb him and Sandy so late at night. She also didn't want to call SAC Bracket because he would give her a short dressing down and tell her to wait for backup.

But there was nothing suggesting she needed backup. She was just going to find a witness. Or at least that was what she was telling herself. In her heart she knew Melinda was in the area where Peggy Bishop lived, and she knew she would not sleep at all were she to wait.

Peggy had called her after all, maybe because she had, she herself was now in danger. Carrie knew she was talking herself firmer into her decision. Once she had made that decision, she wanted to have all the reasons why it had been a good choice.

The man's body they had found at the gas station, Joseph Savage, had led nowhere so far. In her gut, she felt that the instigator of these abductions was skilled at staying in the shadows and using others desperate for a quick buck to do their dirty work. She was equally certain they may never find them, either.

The next best thing was to find the girls. Maybe the person who was holding Melinda would have some answers. They may be able to provide a point of contact which could result in a lead. She knew that only her hard work and determination would save this girl.

As she drove in the moonlit night, Carrie's thoughts drifted back to Sherri and her visit just a few days prior. Something about the woman brought irrational irritation to Carrie. She was just too calm, too happy, and to Carrie no one normal was like that.

And what about her confidence that Melinda would be okay? *How could she know that?* She replayed the scene over and over in her head. As Sherri was walking away, she had turned to look at Carrie and with confidence said that the girl was going to be alright. Carrie felt anger flush through her, then she questioned herself. *Why does that make me so angry?*

When she had prayed for her parents to be okay immediately upon hearing of the car wreck, they had been empty and useless words. God could have spared at least one of them, but he had stripped her completely of her precious parents.

The more her mind ground on those thoughts, the angrier and more determined she became that she and she alone would find these girls.

Chapter Twenty-One

The nearly two-hour drive had lulled Carrie into a relaxed need for sleep. She had fought falling asleep for that last hour, but had finally arrived at the dirt road that lead to Peggy Bishop's house.

The moon that had been so bright during her drive, was now somewhat obscure behind her, and no longer lighting her way. On the map she had seen how remote and wooded this area was, but now that she was actually here, the reality fully hit her. She had left the paved road over four miles ago and had been on a rough gravel road ever since.

As she sat on the side of the narrow gravel road next to the dirt drive that would take her to Peggy's house, she surveyed the area. Across from her there was a bit of a clearing, as best as she could tell, with a rickety old fence around it. It had long since been capable of holding anything in.

The woods consisted of various elm and brush oak trees and tons of undergrowth. It would be very difficult for anyone to walk through without getting cut to shreds by brambles and other bushes.

Carrie jumped and reached for her side arm as the sharp howl of coyotes echoed through the quiet night. Not only was the sound close, but there were many that echoed along. She put her car in drive and turned down the dark dirt road.

The tree canopy engulfed the road within just a dozen or so yards, shutting out any moonlight. Carrie shivered as the dark night gave her an ominous feeling. She crept along in her car looking for any sign that would give her a clue about why Peggy Bishop had called her about Melinda. What had she known? What could she have seen?

After about three miles of the red dirt road, a small white farmhouse reflected the moonlight in its small clearing. It was now nearing midnight, and it made sense that there would be no lights on. There were a couple of old outbuildings, a shed of some type, and an old barn, both with weathered wood. They were clearly kept up but still in need of some repairs.

Carrie had stopped at the end of the road, leaving several yards to the house. She liked the idea of her car being camouflaged in the darkness. She carefully opened her door, trying to stay as quiet as possible.

Then it hit her how absurd it was that here she was at midnight to question a potential witness, even one in potential danger. She knew in reality she had come to find Melinda, but she needed to talk to Peggy or she would never find the girl. If she woke her, she would catch hell in the morning from Bracket and Randy. She might make the woman so angry that she wouldn't even talk to her.

But something was driving her on. Her gut was telling her she should just take a quick look around. There didn't appear to be any pets. No barking dogs or chickens clucking. She walked further out into the small clearing where the moon shone down.

As she stood looking over each area, she realized she did not see a vehicle of any kind. In the barn? She headed to look through the space where the barn doors did not come completely together. The interior of the barn was hidden in darkness and looking through the gap in the doors, all Carrie saw was an expanse of black.

Just as Carrie was turning back toward the house, she felt a large flat metal object whack her upside her head, plummeting her to the ground. Her ears were ringing, and she was dizzy from the shock of the blow.

"Who are you, and what are you doing here?"

"I'm Carrie Border with the OSBI. A lady named Peggy Bishop left me a message about a girl named Melinda."

A lady, presumabley Peggy, stood looking at Carrie as if she were deciding whether or not to believe her story. "It's midnight. If you were law enforcement, you wouldn't be here this time of night and you wouldn't be snooping around my barn."

"I got your message late, and I tried to call you several times. You didn't answer, so I got concerned about you too." Carrie hoped her show of concern would make it more palatable for the woman. Yet, she still stood by, just staring at Carrie with the shovel in her hand. Carrie stayed on the ground where she had fallen, too dizzy to get up.

"Are you Peggy Bishop?" Carrie asked.

"I am." The woman had a hard look on her face and from what Carrie could see in the dark, her eyes were piercing a hole right through her.

Blood trickled down Carrie's cheek and she reached up to feel her head. Pain shot through the tender part of her skull just over her ear. Her hair was matted with blood and Carrie couldn't bear to touch it. Even in the dark, she could tell her vision was blurry.

She rose up on one elbow. "Watch it now," the lady said.

"I'm not here to hurt you. I just came to find Melinda and help you if you needed it."

Peggy appeared to be stoic and calm on the outside, but she

had just clocked an OSBI agent on the head after being party to a young girl's abduction. Inside, she was anything but calm. "So you say."

"Let me get my badge so you can see," offered Carrie. She pushed herself up onto her knees and reached for her badge, surprised that it wasn't there. She tried to look around her in the scruffy grass, but her head throbbed and her vision continued to blur.

"Well, where is it?"

"I guess it fell off when you hit me." Carrie kept trying to focus and feel in the grass. As she was scooting her hand across the ground, she ran the outside of her hand straight into a broken pane of glass, slicing the side of her hand. Jerking it back, she fell backwards, which jarred her throbbing head.

She laid back on the ground, holding her bleeding hand and listening to the rush in her ears from the contusion. She could do nothing but lie there and hope that she recovered quickly.

~

The next morning, Randy called Carrie on his way to the office. She didn't answer, but he thought she might be on another call. It was a good day and Randy was in a great mood. Sandy was pregnant with their first child and she was healthy.

As soon as he walked through the door, his eyes scanned the room for Carrie. When he didn't see her, he recalled he hadn't seen her car in the parking lot. Realizing it was still a bit early, he got right to work at his desk.

He was completing reports on another case he had assisted on that was now heading to court. He wanted to make sure the file was in complete order. When he finally looked up, it was midmorning and Carrie still had not made an appearance.

Suddenly very concerned, Randy popped up out of his chair,

sending it rolling backwards. "Has anyone seen or heard from Carrie this morning?" He called out to the few others in the room. They met his question with a few blank faces and head shakes.

Hurrying to SAC Bracket's office, he stuck his head around the corner. Bracket looked up with a question on his face.

"Have you heard from Carrie this morning? I tried to call her on my drive in and didn't reach her. I got busy with a case file and just realized she still isn't here." He was dialing his cell phone as he spoke.

Bracket stood up from behind his desk and watched as Randy listened to first ringing and then a voicemail message. "Carrie, this is Randy. Where are you? Call me."

He looked up at Bracket. "Go to her house. Let me know what you find."

Randy rushed out the door and drove as quickly as possible to Carrie's house. Her car was not in her drive and the lights were all off. He stood on her front porch, surveying the neighborhood. In desperation, he pulled out his phone and tried to call her again, reaching her voicemail message once more.

"She wasn't at her home and her car isn't there," said Randy in a near panic to Bracket on his ride back to the office.

"Do we know if she is in distress?" Bracket asked.

"Not for certain, but what if she is and we wait?"

"Okay. I will put out a bulletin and pray it is something simple."

Once back in the office, Randy stood looking at Carrie's desk. He picked up the missing girl's case file and opened the folder. A two inch sticky note, that had lost its stickiness, floated from inside the folder to the floor.

Randy didn't notice its escape when it slid out from the bottom of the folder. As he shuffled his feet to sit down, the note flew further under the desk.

Chapter Twenty-Two

As the dark of night gave way to a new day, Carrie lay in the barn, holding her cut hand and attempting to lie still enough to force her head to stop throbbing. She had thrown up twice, and each time wished she had not stopped to eat.

Not long after Peggy had forced her into the barn and chained the door shut, she had tried to look around, but her head injury prevented her from moving very far. With the blackness of the interior, she could see nothing from where she lay.

In the stillness, Carrie could hear a slight rustling. Her ears strained to hear and then a slight squeak pierced the silence. When others joined in, she realized that barn mice, or maybe rats, were lurking not far away. She had to get out of here.

She had made so many mistakes, the greatest of which was coming out here in the first place without Randy or another agent. The second one was not letting them know where she was. Then she had left her phone in the car. It wasn't her fault that her badge had gone flying off when Peggy had hit her, but she felt like it was, nonetheless. She had been so arrogant and foolish to think she could do this on her own.

The blackness of the barn had gained a hint of grayness as morning said hello. Carrie slowly turned her head to look around. Just an old barn and nothing of note. An old junky pickup was parked towards the back with the hood up. *That must be her vehicle, but it looks like it doesn't run.*

Turning her head had not sent her reeling as badly again, so she thought she would try to stand. She had held her cut hand all night with her other one to staunch the bleeding. Now her hands were glued shut with the dried blood. Dare she try to pull them apart?

Deciding to wait until she was up to address her hand, she held them to her chest and gently rolled onto her side and then over onto her stomach. She stopped just for a moment to rest her head on the dirt floor of the barn, then turned just enough to pull up one leg, positioning it underneath her. Pushing down on that knee, it lifted her enough to pull the other one up.

With her lower body elevated above her head, the blood once again rushed in and everything whirled around her. She shut her eyes against the threatening blackness. With both hands still held together, she pushed herself up off of the floor so that her head was level with the rest of her body. She was then able to sit back on her haunches.

The effort to gain that ground was almost more than Carrie could stand. She hurt all over. Her head still throbbed violently, and so did her hand. She just wanted to lie back down, but forced herself to keep moving. She looked down at her blood bundled hands. With that much blood, she knew the cut had been deep.

She pulled one leg up and out, placing her foot on the floor. She pushed hard and planted her other foot beside it. Her vision was considerably better, but there was still some blurriness. She walked over to the gap in the doors and looked out, seeing her badge glinting from the rising sun near the bloody broken glass pane.

Realization that something else didn't feel right made her hands fly to her right side. Her holster was empty. How and when had that happened? Had Peggy taken it off of her in the scuffle?

She needed at least one hand, so she looked around and thought about something to wrap her cut hand in. Everything was caked in layers of grit and grime. The cleanest thing in the barn was her, and she was a sad sight. She could rip a part of her shirt loose and use that, but she would have to separate her hands first.

Tenderly, she tried to pull them apart. They resisted, so she bent into her cupped hands and spit as much saliva as she could wring from her dry mouth. The saliva began wetting the dried blood and loosening its hold. Carrie very carefully pulled them apart a little at a time as the saliva dissolved more and more dried blood.

The last bit was still stuck tight and there was nothing else she could do. So she pulled her hands quickly apart and reached for the hem of her button-up shirt in one swift movement. Blood spurted out as she tried to rip her shirt with her one good hand. The placket in the front would not tear, so she pulled at the shirt, popping the buttons and pulling it off. She wrapped the entire shirt around her hand, which was once again bleeding profusely.

Now for an idea of how to get out of here. Peggy had replaced the chain through the door handles in the front and padlocked them together. Carrie pushed on the doors. Even though they looked decrepit, they held fast against her advances.

Against one wall was an old workbench with odd bits of old tools. Maybe there was something there. As she was rifling through the mishmash of rusty bits, the chain rattled. Carrie whirled around to see Peggy opening the barn doors. She no longer held a shovel or was dressed in her bathrobe.

Peggy stood just inside the barn looking at Carrie and, to her surprise, tears ran down the woman's face. Carrie hoped this was a good sign and that the woman would give her some medical help, then help them find Melinda.

"I am sorry," said Peggy.

Carrie walked towards Peggy. "It's okay. I understand. You didn't know who I was."

Peggy didn't respond, but simply pulled the missing gun from the back of her waistband and held it on Carrie. "March."

"Huh?" Carrie was confused. Was her mind playing tricks on her from the injury?

"Come on. March." Peggy backed around and made way for Carrie to exit the barn. "Keep going."

The morning air was chilly on Carrie's skin with only her sports bra on. Her skin responded by dimpling up, and she wrapped her arms around herself. "Where are we going?"

"Just keep walking that way." Peggy motioned with her head toward the woods behind the barn.

Carrie played along with the woman, waiting for the right moment when she could overtake her. She was a sad mess in which to do that, but at the right time, the woman would be no match for Carrie.

"Peggy, like I said, I am only here because you called and left a message about Melinda. I need to find her." Carrie waited, but Peggy didn't respond.

"What do you know about her disappearance?" Still no response. Carrie looked back and was met with angry, but sad, eyes.

"Turn around and keep walking." Peggy had called and left the message in a moment of weakness when she realized that she needed to let Melinda go. When Melinda had walked out the door, Peggy panicked and unplugged her phone once again, covering the answering machine with a stack of newspapers.

They walked through the woods and then through a small meadow. Carrie did not know how long they had walked, but in her condition, it seemed like an hour or more, and certainly more than she was physically capable of.

"Stop."

Carrie stopped walking and shut her eyes. It felt like she was on the brink of passing out. Her head throbbed where Peggy had hit her with the shovel, and blood caked the side of her face and hair. She looked down at the shirt wrapped around her hands which was filling with more blood.

Peggy walked around and ahead of Carrie. "Come here. Get in the box." She motioned with Carrie's gun towards a metal box in the earth, flush with the ground.

Carrie's mouth hung open. "What do you mean, get in the box?" She was incredulous at the suggestion.

"Get... in... the... box." Peggy took a hard stance with both her hands on the pistol. She meant business.

"Why are you doing this to me?" Carrie screamed.

Carrie weighed her options. She thought she could overtake the woman even in her impaired condition, but she doubted she would survive a gunshot at such close range. However, locked in a metal box in the middle of nowhere as the day grew warmer was also a death sentence.

"Okay. Okay," Carrie said as she stepped first one foot in the box and then the other. It was a very small box, and Carrie wasn't sure she would fit. "I don't think it is big enough."

"You'll fit. Get down in there." Peggy waved the gun.

Carrie sat down. Her mind was racing, attempting to come up with an idea of what to do. Her head throbbed as she thought to lunge at the woman and overpower her, but Carrie was fading and she knew it. She also knew that if she went into the box in her condition, she would likely never come out alive.

In too much pain and too tired to fight any longer, she laid down. She couldn't stretch her legs out, so her knees protruded up above the rim of the box. The woman came around and with her foot, thrust Carrie's knees to one side and slammed the box lid shut.

Carrie heard metal against metal and realized that Peggy had just locked the lid of the box. She knew she would never escape the box on her own.

~

Mining the file for clues to where Carrie could be was fruitless. Randy had logged into her computer and looked through her emails and all the other places he could think to look.

Bracket walked up to him with a grim face. "Anything?"

"Nothing."

Randy rolled Carrie's chair that he had been sitting in backwards to stretch. As he did, it revealed a bright yellow sticky note on the floor underneath their desks. Bracket reached down and picked it up.

Upon reading it, he handed it to Randy. "Have you read this?"

Randy jerked the note from Bracket and scanned it. He looked up at Bracket. "That is where she is. She must have gone to go find this lady."

"Why wouldn't she just call her?"

"I don't know, we need her phone records, since we pinged it and got nothing. Maybe they will help," Randy said. He hurriedly searched that map to find the ladies location, while Bracket worked to get Carrie's phone records.

"I found the lady. She lives pretty far out east of here. Have you seen anything interesting on Carrie's phone records?"

"Of course it must be dead. There was no ping at all, but the last known location before losing the signal was indeed out east of here. Prior to that, she called the number on that note. Take Agent Finch with you and head out that way. I will keep trying to get a location on her phone should it come back online."

"Will do," Randy said. Thoughts about whether Carrie was okay and wondering at her poor decision to go out in the middle of the night to locate that woman distracted him. He knew she had only been an agent for two years, but he knew she had more sense than that, and it irked him she would do something so reckless.

He quickly got Agent Finch, and they made preparations to head east. It was already ten in the morning and the sun was glaring through their windshield, making it hard to navigate the turnpike to Tulsa.

"Okay, looks like we should exit at Stroud, exit 172. We can go on further to Bristow too. Not sure from the map which one is closer. This old Garmin is on the fritz, so it is no help," said Agent Finch.

"Which exit will put us closer to where it looks like this lady Peggy lives?"

Agent Finch flipped the map to the other side and slid his finger along. "I'm not sure. I don't think it really matters. Exiting at Bristow takes us further north, but then we drop straight south. Exiting at Stroud puts us further west but eliminates more of the northward angle. It is literally straight east of Oklahoma City, but there is no highway going straight east."

Suddenly, the exit sign notifying travelers that the Stroud exit was coming in one mile caused Randy to make a quick decision. Exit, head south and then on east.

Agent Finch navigated Randy with one turn after another. This was a ridiculous path of traveling on one road for a couple of miles, then turning onto another one. It may have been closer per miles, but watching for the continuous turns slowed Randy down considerably. With each demand to slow and turn, his blood pressure increased.

Soon, though, the pitiful town, if you could call it that, of Welty, Oklahoma, appeared before them.

Chapter Twenty-Three

No one had traveled down the road and seen Melinda leaning on the old bridge rail. When the morning sunrise had woken her, she stood up stiff and disheartened. She was thirsty and hungry.

With the morning light, she could see that the bridge was very small and an old metal sign riddled with bullet holes said Wolfe Creek. She looked over the edge to see a small stream trickling underneath the bridge. It ran muddy red and didn't look like anything Melinda should drink, but she was so thirsty.

She raised up from looking over the rail to look up the road first one way, then the other. The road was red dirt and rutted. It looked seldom traveled. She was still in dense woods and she could hear no sounds of civilization anywhere.

Her thirst led her to at least inspect the creek below a bit closer to see if there might be a chance of drinkable water. She stepped around the rail at the end and carefully onto the brush growing on the slope.

Immediately, her modified shoes began to slide in the layers of old leaves and debris. Not being anchored to her heels, they slid from underneath her feet. The unstable movement flung her body to the ground, and she rapidly slid down the slope to the edge of the creek.

Laying still for a moment, she assessed her situation. She was okay. Scraped and littered with dirt and leaves, but still okay. She breathed a sigh of relief and turned to sit on the slope.

From that level, the water appeared a little cleaner, but had a green cast underneath the surface. She realized it was the green moss on the rocks in the water.

She made her way to where the water had cut out a tiny little pool at the side. She bent down and cupped her hands to dip up the water. Red sand swirled in the water, but otherwise it looked clear. *I've probably swallowed this much dirt dry the past two days, so drinking a little bit more won't hurt me.*

She lifted her hands to her mouth and drank. It wasn't much more than a quarter cup, but at least it was wet. She shifted down to the ground to get closer and hopefully better convey the water from stream to mouth.

Just as she was once again raising her hands from the water, movement caught her eye. A dark brown, nearly black snake was coasting towards her down the very narrow stream. Fear froze her there on the ground, with her hands midway between the water and her mouth. *Oh no, it's a water moccasin. It's poisonous.*

As the snake grew closer, it slowed. Melinda remained frozen. Her heart was pounding in her ears and she didn't know if she should remain still or attempt to run. She knew though, that by the time she attempted to jump up from where she was and run, the snake would have already struck. While she was debating her fate, the snake soon moved on, uninterested.

Melinda collapsed on the side of the creek in tears.

"This is it?" Randy drove through the location of Welty before he realized they had arrived. "There is nothing here!"

He turned their SUV back around and drove slowly to where county road N3700 intersected going north, and turned. They crept along, seeing a few homes, some really nice, at random distances apart. There was no post office, no gas station or store of any kind.

They moved further north from where the map said Welty was. The map said Welty was at the intersection of county road N3700, which they were on, and county road E96, which they had been on. Finally, Randy turned the SUV around on a dirt road to head back south.

Deep drifts of sand had blown onto the portion of dirt road where it met the edge of the hard-packed gravel of N3700. The sand took Randy by surprise as the SUV caught and skidded sideways. The drifts were much deeper than they appeared to be and the tires merely continued to dig and scatter sheets of red Oklahoma sand.

Randy paused and shifted the SUV into a lower gear and once again attempted to dislodge them. He had to admit, he had little-to-no experience traveling these old dirt roads.

Finally, he shoved it back into park and they both exited the vehicle. Randy reached down to feel the sand. It was nothing like you would lay your towel on at the beach to enjoy a summer day by the ocean. This sand was slightly red and incredibly fine. It sifted through Randy's finger like extra fine sugar.

He dropped his hand and attempted to walk around to the side where the front passenger wheel was losing its battle. With each step, heaps of the fine sand rushed into his shoes. Agent Finch watched quietly as Randy walked around the SUV.

"What the hell?" Randy was furious and the scorching sun was bearing down, which caused rivulets of sand-laden sweat to drip into his eyes.

"I used to live in the country on old roads like this. They are a beast. If we can dig here to free up this wheel some, then back around that way, I think we can get out," offered Agent Finch. Frustrated and angry, Randy nodded.

After digging with Agent Finch in the shifting sand for what seemed like an hour, Randy said, "Okay. You drive."

Randy sat in the passenger seat with the door open. He took his shoes off one by one and attempted to empty them of the sand. The breeze caught the fine particles and spun them back inside the SUV. Randy was a patient person, but he was nearing his limit.

The sun was reflecting off of the hot dirt road and the noise of the insects was nearly deafening. There hadn't been one vehicle pass by the entire time they had been working to get back on the gravel road.

Agent Finch looked over at Randy and contemplated what to say. He knew Randy was anxious about his partner Carrie, and the more anxious he got, the worse their situation became. "Take a deep breath and calm down. We will get to her. She is a good agent and she will be fine until we find her."

Randy nodded. "Yes, she is a good agent, but sometimes she doesn't think responsibly and rushes ahead too fast. I'm sure with time she will become wiser, if she lives that long."

Agent Finch put the SUV in gear, cut the wheel just right, and gently pressed the gas. At first, he felt the same resistance from the sand, but then it suddenly caught hold and rolled forward. They both breathed a collective sigh of relief when they were firmly back on solid ground.

"I hoped that there would be a store or gas station in Welty where we could ask if they knew this Peggy, and then they could give us exact directions to her house," said Randy.

"Well, let's get back to where this road meets the other one and we can try calling her again."

Carrie's phone went straight to voicemail. Randy knew that

meant it was dead or off, just as it had been all day. Peggy's phone rang and rang too, and no one answered and no answering machine picked up.

"Okay, well, let's see if we can find her."

Emily laid on the sofa in complete despair. She had cried until her eyelids felt like sandpaper rubbing against her eyes. She tried not to think about her foot and the horrible poison that was creeping up her leg and into her bloodstream. But it was impossible.

When the tears had finally subsided because there were no more left to cry, she laid numb on the sofa. Against her will, self preservation kicked in and she thought of ways she could rescue herself.

She raised her head just enough to look around the room. If there was a phone, she might crawl to it and call someone. She saw nothing. *But there has to be a phone. Who doesn't have a phone?*

Her body revolted in earnest as she pushed herself up on one elbow. She grit her teeth to bear the pain. It took her breath away, but finally she was up with her good leg dangling off the sofa onto the floor. She was up as far as she could go, resting on one arm.

There was a half wall between the living room and kitchen, but no sign of a wall phone. There was none in the living room either. She couldn't remember hearing a phone ring the entire time she had been there. *Maybe she has a cell phone.*

Emily pulled her injured leg towards her on the sofa in an effort to sit upright. She screamed out in pain. Little specks floated before her eyes as she fought to keep from passing out.

I can't walk on this leg. I can't even drag it. What am I going to do?

Suddenly, in the distance, she thought she heard an engine, a car or a truck. It was faint, but maybe, just maybe, there was someone else coming.

Her eyes darted about frantically, thinking of what to do and how to do it. She would just have to bear the pain or lay here and die.

She braced herself by putting one hand on the floor. As she moved to slide herself to the floor, pain once again ripped through her body. *I have to keep going.*

Taking a deep breath, she pulled her injured leg down to the floor. It felt as though she had no control over it. It already felt dead to her, and she knew in reality it was quickly becoming so.

She allowed herself a few more deep breaths to recover before attempting to drag herself to the front door. The engine noise was still present, but she couldn't tell if it had grown louder. She knew she had to hurry or it might drive away.

Dragging herself across the floor with her arms and elbows was the hardest thing she had ever done. The ten feet to the door might as well have been two hundred. Finally, she was there. She looked up at the doorknob, which seemed miles above her.

I have to stand up. I have to get to the doorknob. It took every ounce of strength she had, but using her arms against the door jamb, she worked to move her one good leg beneath her. The effort increased the pain. Blackness threatened to take her under. The flickering specks were now shades of darkness.

In one final thrust, she reached for the knob and turned it. By the time the door opened, the blackness had completely engulfed her. She never felt her body crash onto the rickety wooden deck.

Chapter Twenty-Four

Finding Peggy's was challenging. Randy wasn't sure he had ever seen such a remote location for a home. They had taken several roads, backtracked, nearly got stuck in the sand again, and finally found a narrow overgrown drive.

The drive had to have been at least four miles long, and the wild nature of it suggested that it was rarely traveled. The SUV bounced and creaked as it hit first one rut, then another. They were creeping along at a snail's pace, viewing nothing but dense woods on each side.

Gradually, a clearing appeared which revealed a small white frame house that had seen better days. There were no vehicles, only an old weathered wood barn in the back and a couple of other old out buildings.

"I guess this is it, but I don't see any vehicles, including Carrie's," said Randy.

Agent Finch slowed to a stop and turned the key. "Feels deserted."

Eager to stretch and even more eager to find Carrie, the agents exited the SUV. The door that faced the drive appeared to be a back or side door. "You go around to the front and knock. I'll wait here and knock if no one answers you," said Randy.

Agent Finch stepped onto the ancient front porch and his firm knock rattled the old screen door. Silence echoed through the house, so he opened the screen door and pounded on the front door. "This is Agent Finch with the OSBI. Please open the door." Still nothing but silence.

Randy could hear that Agent Finch was not receiving any response, so he too, did the same. "Please open up. This is a law enforcement matter, and it is urgent."

Neither agent heard anything. Agent Finch walked back around to meet up with Randy. "What do you say we look around?"

"Exactly what I was thinking," replied Randy. "I know Carrie's car isn't here, but I feel like she must have been here since this appeared to be where she was heading. What if we got it all wrong?"

Squatting down to look at the red sand piled in the drive, Agent Finch spotted several sets of car tracks. "Look here. These look like tracks from the tires that would be on Carrie's car. They came and left." He looked over at Randy, who had squatted beside him.

"She was here. What if she came, and either talked to Peggy and left, or just left because Peggy wasn't home?"

"Then where is she now?"

Randy stood and looked around. "I don't know."

The two men stood and began to walk towards the old barn. Randy was looking at the grass and weeds. It looked as though it was rarely, if ever, mowed. But it also looked as though it was not watered intentionally, with bare patches everywhere and stunted growth.

Suddenly, a familiar object caught Randy's eye, and he quickly bent down. "James, here is Carrie's badge. Would you go get some evidence bags and the camera from the SUV?"

Agent Finch sprinted off obediently to retrieve the items from their vehicle. He returned quickly, panting slightly as he handed them to Randy.

They needed to treat her badge as evidence, so he handled it with a pair of latex gloves and took pictures of where it lay.

"Look, here's blood." Agent Finch pointed to the broken pane of glass that Carrie had cut her hand on.

Randy took more pictures and gently separated the blood-stained piece of glass from the dirt and dried grass. After placing the glass in a paper evidence bag, they knew there was a story here. Finding Carrie's badge gave them full authority to search the property at will.

Since the badge was found so close to the barn, they approached it on high alert, weapons drawn. Peggy had replaced the chain through the old rusty door handles and secured it with a padlock yet again.

"What now?" asked Agent Finch. "We would have to destroy the door to get inside."

Randy peered in through the crack between the doors. Even in broad daylight, it was pitch dark inside. "Carrie," he called out. No answer.

"Let's check the house. Maybe we can get in there easier than the barn. And we might even find a key to the lock," said Randy.

Sure enough, the back door was unlocked. "Ironic that the house is unlocked, and the barn is secure," said Agent Finch.

"Yes. Makes me wonder what she is hiding in the barn."

"As far out as we are, I'm surprised she would lock anything."

When they stepped into the kitchen from outside, Randy once again called out, notifying anyone in earshot that an OSBI agent had entered the premises. No answer.

The house was tidy. It looked like an old lady lived there.

Crocheted doilies were draped on all the furniture and ruffled curtains hung at the windows. Everything was old, but had been well taken care of.

Randy noticed a pile of newspapers that sat on the end of the kitchen counter that appeared to have something bulky underneath. When he removed the newspapers there sat Peggy's phone and answering machine, both unplugged from the wall.

"No wonder she didn't answer the phone."

The agents walked through the house, calling out first Carrie's name, then Peggy's. Nothing seemed amiss. At the pink bedroom, they paused. Folded on the dresser were a pair of girls' jeans and a shirt. Randy lifted the shirt and showed it to Agent Finch.

"Isn't this what Melinda was wearing when she disappeared?"

Agent Finch pulled out a flyer from his pocket with Melinda's picture and last seen description on it. He held it out for Randy to see. "Yes, I believe it is."

Melinda was exhausted, frustrated, hungry, and hurting. She was a strong girl made of fortitude, but every person had their limits and she felt she had reached hers. The blisters on the backs of her heels had burst in the night and they were looking raw and angry, possibly growing infected. Her shoes were ruined and useless at this point.

After using the last of her energy to climb back up onto the road, she looked around. She knew where she had come from, but should she continue or backtrack? She didn't know where to go or what to do.

Finally, she decided to go in the direction she had been going. As she walked, she thought about Peggy. She honestly felt sorry for the lonely lady. She also felt relieved that she had allowed her to leave, but leaving had seemed to do her no good. Was she walking in circles or actually making progress? She didn't know.

After about a half mile, she came to a narrow dirt road that snaked off to her left through the woods. She paused and considered that it might go to someone's house and maybe they could help her. But what kind of person would she find down that road? She didn't know, but she knew she had to take a chance and see.

With renewed energy, Melinda turned and headed up the narrow road. Just like Peggy's drive had been long and overgrown, so was this one. Unlike Peggy's, though, this one was winding. Melinda lost track of time, but after some time, instead of coming to a house, she came to a clearing next to a river.

The river ran red and flowed heavy, surging past Melinda. It was narrow, but high, and looked treacherous.

There was old fishing tackle scattered over on the side of the bank, next to a dilapidated old folding chair with the webbing half gone. Melinda's shoulders slumped, and she cried out in earnest. She crumpled to the ground and curled up in a ball and sobbed.

What am I going to do? She cried to herself, for there was no one else to hear.

~

As Buck pulled up to the old trailer home, he noticed the front door was wide open. The hair on the back of his neck stood up. Something was not right. As he pulled closer, it looked like a pile of clothing was lying on the front deck.

He didn't know who lived here, but his dog had run off and he was checking every house in the area to see if anyone had seen him. The proximity of this house back in the woods nearly prevented him from turning down the washed out dirt road. But he knew it would forever bug him if he didn't check them all.

The old engine clicked in the quiet when he turned the key off. The heat bore down and insects sang. A grasshopper landed on his cheek. Startled, he quickly swatted it away and shuddered. He hated feeling their itchy little feet.

Taking his time, he stood by the truck and did a full 180 reconnoissance around the property. It hadn't been very well-cared for. Tall grass grew everywhere. Scrub pines and cedars that should have been cleared out were not. An old shed near the back had broken out windows and a slight lean to it.

He began walking towards the front deck. As he grew closer, he saw that the pile of clothing on the front deck was not that at all, but a person, a young girl.

"Miss," Buck gently shook the girl. "Miss." Alarmed at no response, he pressed two fingers to her neck. Feeling a pulse, he let out a sigh of relief and renewed his efforts to revive the girl, but there was no reaction.

Knowing he had to get her help, he stood to find a phone in the house. It was hot inside and there was a wretched stench. He looked around for a phone and finally found one under a pile of old rags in the kitchen. There was no dial tone.

Curious about the smell, he carefully walked towards the back of the trailer, only to discover its source. A woman lay sprawled backwards on an old mattress with a gun in her hand. The horror of the situation, a suicide and a nearly dead young girl, gripped Buck and he turned and ran.

Maybe he could get the girl to the hospital and contact the sheriff there. Back on the porch, he turned the girl over and scooped her up in his arms. As he did, he noticed her ankle. Red and purple splotched with angry red lines creeping up her leg. The urgency of her situation fueled his increasing anxiety.

At the truck, he opened the back door and laid her in the backseat. He didn't have any blankets or substitutes to cushion her.

The seat would have to do. They were miles from the nearest hospital and he knew time was not this girl's friend at the moment.

Once off the dirt drive and on the paved road, he gunned the engine and headed east towards town. Normally it would take an hour, but today he hoped it would take much less time.

Chapter Twenty-Five

As soon as they knew that this was where Melinda had been, they called SAC Bracket and had him contact the local sheriff. It would take about forty-five minutes for them to arrive at their remote location. They also put an APB out for Carrie's car. Their assumption was that Peggy had the car and probably Melinda with her. But where was Carrie?

Agent Finch, now viewing the inside of the house from a different perspective, searched for clues and other signs that Melinda had indeed been there, and where they might have gone. In the living room, he noticed what looked like two crochet projects.

"This is weird," Agent Finch said.

"What?" Randy asked as he walked up beside James.

"There are two crochet projects as if not just Peggy, but also Melinda, was crocheting." He looked over at Randy.

"That would maybe say that the girl was comfortable here. Do you think she knew Peggy? Maybe an aunt or something? We need to have Bracket check with the Banners to see if they know a Peggy Bishop."

Agent Finch relayed the message to Bracket and resumed his purview of the house. It was small and old but very tidy, as they had noticed at first glance. So tidy that there was nothing out that would further indicate that two people were here. There were no dishes on the drainboard. No other clothing lying about. There were also no personal objects that would indicate a young girl was here.

"Well, we need to find Carrie. When the sheriff gets here, he and the crime scene techs can handle the house. I'm worried that Peggy has harmed Carrie and she may need medical attention." Randy was thinking of the blood on the broken glass near where they had found her badge. It didn't look to be that old.

"Did you see any signs of a padlock key?" asked Randy.

Agent Finch shook his head. "But then I haven't been specifically looking for that either." They began urgently opening kitchen drawers, looking for any keys at all, but found none. Randy looked around the room, wondering where Peggy would have kept the key to the padlock. The thought occurred to him she might even have it with her. Noticing the door at the back of the kitchen, he opened it to find a small laundry room. As his eyes adjusted, he noticed a small wooden key holder on the back wall. Only one set of keys hung there.

In two swift steps, Randy had crossed the room and retrieved the keys. By the time he hit the back door, it was in a near run. If Carrie was in the barn unconscious, he would get to her as quickly as possible.

The key proved to be the correct one and slid the mechanism quickly to release the latch. The door tried to resist along the dirt floor, but Randy pushed even harder. Tree canopy from outside kept the sunlight from filtering into the old barn. It appeared virtually empty.

"Carrie," Randy called out, working his way along the outer walls. Agent Finch had joined him and was doing the same.

"Randy, look here."

There was a puddle of blood. Not far away were two areas of vomit. "Vomit," mused Randy. "What would cause her to vomit?"

"A head injury. A concussion." Randy looked at Agent Finch. They both suspected that Peggy had hit Carrie, causing a concussion, and she had cut her hand on the glass. Two serious injuries that would need immediate attention.

Melinda had sat for what seemed like hours. Her forehead rested on her knees with her hands hugging her legs to her. She was exhausted and out of tears. She had no idea what to do.

"God, help me please," Melinda prayed. The only other time in her life she had prayed was when she was trapped in the box. She had prayed to be let out, and she had been. Maybe if she prayed again, it would work again.

Lifting her head and resting her chin on her knees, she watched as the red dirt rushed by in the river. Ugly. *Why can't Oklahoma have beautiful clear rivers?* It was at least peaceful by the edge of the river in the shade. Birds rustled about and a cooling breeze blew through. *If I sit here long enough, will someone come back to fish and find me?*

She glanced over at the discarded fishing tackle and old chair now and realized that it could have been there for years. The road here was overgrown and Melinda knew it was rarely traveled. But she had been walking for hours, days even, and was getting nowhere. She had come to the realization that she had probably been walking in circles. It was clear to her she was in a densely wooded area with little to no population.

Plop. Plop plop. Melinda looked up and a large raindrop hit her square on her cheek. *Oh no! Now it is going to rain.* The sky was a mix of dark clouds and sunlight. *Hopefully, there will only be a few sprinkles.*

As Melinda watched, a large flat section of wood floated by. Someone had secured together several wide boards, and they were floating along like a raft. It swiveled around and the corner shifted up and caught on a huge tuft of water grass. It rocked stationary on the edge of the river, yearning to move on but unable to do so.

An idea came to Melinda, but seemed ludicrous to her. *Can I float out of here?* The thought brought her terror, and she shuddered. *Would floating down the river bring me to civilization quicker, or would I drown in the process?*

She stood and walked over to the edge of the boards. The river was fairly narrow at this point and when she looked downriver, it appeared to be wider and to calm down. Her tattered shoes had stretched and torn as she had walked on the sand. She could barely hold her feet in them any longer.

The lure of the raft grew stronger. She lifted the corner and saw three additional boards holding the top section securely. *I think I can do this.*

She pulled the makeshift raft up and over to where it was no longer caught on the grass and was half in the water and half out. Melinda placed one hand on each side of the raft and pushed. As she pushed it firmly into the water, she jumped on top of it. She pulled her legs from underneath her and sat cross-legged, holding onto the sides.

The rush was terrifyingly exhilarating. And then the rain began in earnest.

~

The trip to the hospital had taken much less time because Buck had pushed his truck to the maximum. There was still no sign of life from the girl in the back seat, and he wasn't even sure she was still breathing. He thought of his own daughter at home and what if it were her?

He flew into the emergency portico, slammed the truck into park, and jumped out. He scooped the girl in his arms and ran towards the glass doors. With a swoosh, the doors welcomed him and he continued to run to find help.

A medical team quickly nestled her onto a gurney with ample care. Buck leaned over with his hands anchored to his knees as he attempted to gain his breath and composure.

"Sir," a lady was standing there with a clipboard. He looked up, knowing she needed information, and nodded.

His first comment was about the lady in the trailer and how the Sheriff needed to go check it all out. There was something sincerely wrong about the entire scene. The lady stopped in her pursuit of information gathering and called the sheriff. She put Buck on the phone and he explained the entire situation. The lady was taking notes.

The sheriff finally ended the call, and the lady began her questioning. Buck knew nothing beyond what he had told the sheriff, so he could add nothing to the lady's forms. Remembering his truck was still running, he excused himself and went to move it to the parking lot.

The medical team was quickly tending to Emily. Her vitals were low, and they couldn't bring her to consciousness. Their greatest concern, though, was her ankle. Why had it gone untreated for so long? It was apparent that she needed surgery immediately.

When Buck re-entered the emergency waiting room, a new nurse with a clipboard met him, asking about Emily's next of kin. They needed approval to do surgery. He knew nothing and merely shook his head. "I don't know who she is or who her people are."

Since it was clearly a life or death situation, the medical staff had no other option but surgery. They hoped they would not have to amputate, and even if they did, that the poison had not permeated her body to the point of not being able save her at all.

Buck used the payphone to call his wife and explain where he was and what had happened. He didn't feel right leaving the young girl alone just yet. She was in surgery and in his heart he knew he needed to stay and see this through.

The surgery took several hours. Buck paced the floor and thumbed through every magazine. The television held no allure to him, but out of sheer boredom, he tried. Finally, a surgeon came out and walked over to Buck. Fatigue had adhered to his face and limbs.

"Are you the man who brought her in?" Buck nodded.

"She came through surgery. We were able to save her leg for now. We had to cut away damaged tissue, and we believe were able to stop the poison from entering her bloodstream. It will take a lot of physical therapy for her to get back on track and learn to walk again, but we have high hopes."

Relief rushed through Buck, and he broke out in a smile. He had saved her, and that felt good. "Thank you, doctor. Thank you." Buck took the doctor's hand in both of his and shook it heartily.

"She hasn't woken up yet, but when she does, maybe we can get some critical information from her about who she is and what happened to her. It is fortunate that you were able to bring her here. We have some of the best orthopedic surgeons in the state of Arkansas."

Buck listened. Yes, he was very grateful and felt that he could now leave, knowing the girl was in excellent hands. He left his home phone number with them, asking them to please keep him posted.

When he left, he had no idea that Emily was in a coma, with no indication of how long she would remain there or if she would ever wake from it.

Chapter Twenty-Six

"Peggy could have Carrie in the car with her. She might have taken her to a hospital," said Agent Finch. That seemed doubtful to both of them, but Randy sent a message to Bracket to check all the local hospitals.

"Okay, so if she is not with Peggy, where is she?" asked Randy.

"Maybe she tried to walk out of here."

"Wouldn't we have come across her on our drive in?" Randy's face was pinched in doubt and concern.

Agent Finch stood looking around. "Let's look for tracks. The sand may help us again."

They concentrated their efforts on performing a grid search for more tracks in the sandy drive. What they found were several footprints. Two sets of were distinctly adult size and one was smaller, likely Melinda. The smaller tracks headed down the road away from the house. The two adult tracks went in several directions, but they finally found a trail walking toward the woods.

"Here we go," said Randy. He was feeling energized, but still gravely concerned. What if she had marched Carrie off into the woods and shot her?

The red sand ended at the edge of the woods, and tall grass took its place. They followed along where they saw the grass trampled down for about ten feet, then gave way to rocks and debris from the canopy of trees. They continued to search, but it was clear they had lost their trail.

Car doors slamming at Peggy's house rang through the woods, so they relinquished their search and went back to the house. There, waiting for them, was the county sheriff and a deputy. Introductions were made along with further explanation of what had happened and what they had found. The crime scene techs would come from Oklahoma City and wouldn't arrive for another hour.

The county seat of Okfuskee County was the town of Okeema, which was on the opposite side of the county and quite a distance from Welty. So, Sheriff Anderson knew nothing of Peggy. The entire six hundred and nineteen square miles of the county only had a bit more than eleven thousand residents, of which over three thousand lived in Okeema proper. It was a very large, densely-wooded and sparsely populated county.

"I've got deputies canvasing the local residents. They sent me both a picture of your agent, Carrie Border and the missing girl, Melinda Banner, and each deputy will be showing those pictures. As soon as I hear anything, I will let you know."

"We were searching for tracks. We found two pairs of adult tracks heading up towards those woods, but then lost the trail in the underbrush."

Just then, the sun hid behind a large dark cloud and the heavens opened, drenching everyone and everything beneath it.

Sheriff Anderson and the agents ran towards the house for cover from the rain. They stepped just inside the kitchen and dripped on the old linoleum. "Well, so much for the tracks," said Randy. He was exasperated and not sure what to do next.

While the downpour continued outside, they sat at the kitchen table and took the time to give the sheriff details of their case. He listened carefully and took notes. When Randy had come to the end of the narrative, the sheriff asked, "So, this might not be your typical human trafficking scenario. The girls were stolen, kidnapped, but this girl was sent here to Peggy Bishop, or did Peggy just find her?"

"We aren't sure. That is all we have come up with so far." Agent Finch searched the sheriff's face to hopefully see if anything might resonate with him. They needed valuable input to help them solve this case.

Sheriff Anderson sat quietly for a while, thinking. He was younger than many sheriffs, only thirty-two. But the sheriff prior to him had retired, and he had been the senior deputy. He won the election easily with the retiring sheriff's recommendation. He had gained his approval because he was a good deputy, solving the cases they had with ingenuity rather than brawn.

"It appears that this lady, Peggy, might have bought this girl from someone, somewhere. So, where did she connect with them and where did she get the money from? We need her bank records to see if we can find a connection. I know it is urgent that we find Agent Border and Melinda, but there could be a clue if we can find more," said the sheriff. "Are we sure she didn't just find her?"

"In my gut, I feel she is the perpetrator. Carrie has likely met with foul play here too. It is too much of a coincidence for Peggy to not be involved," said Randy.

The agents nodded. They had been so embroiled in finding Carrie that the other elements of the case had drifted to the back of their minds. Randy pulled out his phone and dialed Bracket. By the end of the day, they would know more.

"The guy that took the girls was obviously a middle-man, but someone else took the money and did the deal." The sheriff looked for an acknowledgment on the agents' faces and their bobbing heads rewarded him.

"We think Carrie has a concussion and a deep cut. We found vomit, which could mean she has a head injury, and we found an old piece of glass next to her badge with blood on it and more blood in the old barn. If it was hers, she could be critical." Randy stood and paced the kitchen.

He glanced over at the phone and plugged the line back in. There was an instant dial-tone. When he re-plugged it and the answering machine in, the red blinking light showed that there were three messages.

Randy looked over at Sheriff Anderson and Agent Finch, who had pulled out his notepad ready to take notes. He pressed the button to retrieve the messages.

Message number one was left two days prior. A man's voice came over the speaker. "We have left your package at the designated coordinates."

Message number two was left three days prior. A woman's voice came over the speaker. "Payment received. We will deliver your package at the designated coordinates tomorrow."

The final message was left two weeks prior. The woman's voice came over the speaker again. "We have received your request for a daughter. Call the number in which you made the request and we will make arrangements for payment and delivery."

Randy's mouth hung open. "We have them, their numbers anyway. Yes! We are getting somewhere. Now we have to find Carrie."

The rain moved over for the sun, which was once again dominating the sky. They walked out the back door and into the yard, only to see ruts where the rain had washed large gouges in the driveway and with it, any evidence they had not been able to find or collect.

~

Melinda hung on for dear life. The river had indeed grown calmer when it had widened out, and she had let out a sigh of relief. But with the rain, the river rose and roared back to life. There was no wind, but with the rocking of the raft, Melinda felt vulnerable sitting up. She maneuvered herself so that she could lie flat on the raft with her arms stretched out to her sides, gripping the boards fiercely.

She laid her cheek on the wet wood and clamped her eyes shut. *Just ride it out. Just ride it out.* She was afraid to look. If something ominous loomed ahead of her, there was nothing she could do about it, anyway. To look would only sow more fear.

Then the rain stopped as abruptly as it had started. The sun warmed Melinda's rain soaked back, and it felt good. The river was still surging rapidly forward, but the raft held steady. Fatigue and the warm sun lulled Melinda to the brink of unconsciousness. She tried to fight it, but slumber crept in and pulled her away.

The box was not sealed and air seeped in around the lip of the lid, but that wasn't what concerned Carrie. Her head throbbed worse than any hangover she had ever had. She felt lightheaded, but thought it was as much from a loss of blood as it was from the concussion. She had heard the lock snap shut and knew that she did not have the physical ability at this moment to overcome it.

The morning air had been cool when Peggy marched her in her sports bra to the box, but now the sun had risen and was high. It was bearing down on the metal box and Carrie felt like she was inside an oven.

When the downpour began, it had awoken Carrie. At first she thought the pounding of raindrops was from someone who had come to rescue her. "Help! Is anyone out there?" she called out.

But when the rain drowned out her words, she knew then it was not a someone, but a something.

Initially, she was thrilled. The rain washed away the relentless heat and managed to cool the box somewhat. But after a good thirty minutes, the hole the box was in was beginning to fill with water and it was rushing up under the lip of the lid and over the side of the box.

Carrie couldn't believe it. She would drown in this box. Knowing she had to get out some how, some way. She had frantically looked when she had first been deposited in the box. It was made well, but was also made for temporary confinement.

As the water poured in, Carrie tried to move first one way, then another. There was no room for flexibility. She couldn't use her hands and she could not get her feet into a position to push against the lid.

What if I can roll over and push up with my back against the lid? Still, there was no way to maneuver into any other position, and all the effort had only succeeded in increasing the throb in her head.

The water was still running steadily into the box and was now up to her ears and mid-shoulder. Years of pent up anger spewed forth and Carrie screamed. She vowed to make better decisions if she should ever escape this mess. But those vows did nothing to help her now.

Chapter Twenty-Seven

Melinda awoke with a start. She raised her head, and the scenery was the same. The red rolling dirty river was still carrying her through dense woodlands. She vowed to stay alert and look for any sign of life, anything that might indicate a place to get help.

She did not know where she was or how far downriver she had come. But she knew at some point there would be somewhere she could find help.

The sun bore down, but it was lowering in the western sky, which was behind her. She was traveling east. In order to try and stay alert, she pulled her legs up and once again sat cross-legged, still holding on to the sides of the raft.

The ride on the river had been relatively smooth despite the surging water. But Melinda sensed the river was changing. She strained her neck to look up ahead. Sound surged through the air and concern prickled her skin.

Suddenly she knew she was in danger, real danger. Just ahead were large boulders protruding from the water, and she had no idea what to do. *Will the small raft survive the boulders and the rapids they caused? What was on the other side?*

She looked frantically to her right and to her left. The sides of the banks were too far for her to reach and she doubted she could swim in this fast current.

There was no time to wonder for long, though. The boulders soon assaulted the small raft and jarred Melinda fiercely. She hung on as it bounced from one boulder to another. Determined, she held on as the rapids threw her from side to side. Large sprays of water showered her and hindered visibility.

Then suddenly, another large boulder slammed the raft and she was flying through the air and into the spray. She hit the water hard, banging her head on a rock. "Help. Help me please." Her quiet words were lost as she floated down the now calm river.

The boys had been told not to go fishing, but their parents were not home, so they went anyway. The small offshoot of the river they favored was much calmer than the main part, so it was easier to catch fish. Honestly, it wasn't about the fish, anyway.

And sure enough, by five in the afternoon, they had still caught nothing.

Laying his rod down, Sean said, "I'm bored. Let's explore a bit." Trevor nodded and did the same. They had explored these woods along the river many times, but they always seemed to find something new.

They walked down to where the river split into the offshoot and stood. The water rolled. "Wow. The water is high today," said Trevor.

"Yeah. I guess because of the rain."

"Hey, what's that?" Trevor pointed upriver to a shape floating towards them on the water. They moved closer to the edge and then realized that was a person.

"Oh no! We have to help her."

"How? We can't go in that water," said Trevor.

"We have to do something."

They knew this area like the back of their hands and so simultaneously they devised a plan. They ran as fast as they could further downriver to where there was an old-washed out bridge. If they could get out on the bridge, they might snag her with a branch.

They barely got there ahead of Melinda, but just in time to shove an old board they had found into the water. It didn't snag her, merely bounced off of her shoulder.

"Dang. What now?" asked Sean.

"We have to go get help." The old bridge began to creak and moan under their feet. A board proved rotten and Sean's foot thrust through. Trevor grabbed Sean's hand and pulled him free. When they looked up, there was no sign of Melinda up ahead.

"You okay? We got to go now."

Sean nodded, and they ran home as fast as they could to get help for the girl in the river, not knowing if she was dead or alive.

Randy had Bracket working on Peggy's phone records and the crime scene techs were combing through every inch of the house and barn.

There seemed to be no record of the coordinates referred to in the phone message. They had looked at every notepad and scrap of paper in the house.

"We are just going to have to comb the woods and surrounding property systematically. We don't know where Carrie is, but we did see tracks leading to the woods. That leads me to believe that she is not with Peggy, but somewhere on the property." Randy had taken charge and was delivering a plan. The other law enforcement personnel nodded in agreement.

The sheriff rolled out a large map he kept in his vehicle. They worked to divide and plot out segments to search.

Just as they were about to take off, the sheriff's radio squelched. "Sheriff. I just got a call from a family on the east side of the county. Their boys were fishing on the Deep Fork river and saw a girl floating on it. They tried to snag her and pull her in, but the river was too tumultuous. She floated downriver, and they ran back to get help. They do not know how far downriver she is right now."

"Is she alive?" asked the sheriff.

"They couldn't tell. She was floating on her back, so there is a good possibility that she is."

"Okay, notify the sheriff of Okmulgee County and see if he can get his deputies out there and search for her. They will be closer than we are. We are still here in Welty searching for the missing agent. Keep me posted."

Randy's mind was sorting through all the information. "Peggy is gone in Carrie's car, we assume. Melinda, we assume, is floating down the Deep Fork River. Carrie must be somewhere in the woods alive or badly injured or she would have found her way back."

"The Sheriff in Okmulgee County is good. They will make quick work of finding the girl. We don't know for sure it is Melinda. It could be any girl," said the Sheriff.

"True, but it seems like a huge coincidence," said Agent Finch. They all nodded in agreement.

"Okay, let's proceed as planned and begin searching for Agent Border."

The Sheriff doled out instructions to the three deputies he had on site and they all set out in search of Carrie. Ahead of them were tangles and dense woods, with only small clearings dotted about here and there. They knew the initial direction the footprints had traveled in, so they convened at the place where they had been no longer visible and fanned out from there.

It was after six o'clock, and Randy's stomach knotted in hunger and in fear. He hoped for the best, but feared the worst.

~

Melinda's head throbbed. She was floating on the river and was moving in and out of consciousness. Earlier she thought she had heard voices and something hard had struck her shoulder, but she wasn't aware enough to know what that had been.

She had nothing left to fight with. If the river took her, so be it.

"There she is!" A voice yelled.

Melinda wondered if she had imagined the voice or if she were dreaming. Then she heard more voices and other unfamiliar noises. She opened her eyes and tried to look around, but from her back, she could see nothing.

Suddenly the sound of a motor grew louder, and beside her loomed a large orange inflatable boat. Then she was being dragged from the water and placed inside.

Her eyes moved, and she blinked to avoid the remaining sun. "She's alive," a voice rang out.

It seemed as though several voices at once were vying for her attention. She was too spent to try and separate out the various questions and formulate a response. She simply closed her eyes and said, "My name is Melinda Banner, and I want to go home."

Chapter Twenty-Eight

Randy and the other law enforcement officials were thrilled to hear that they had pulled Melinda from the river and that she was alive. The search for Carrie was infuriatingly slow. The underbrush in the woods hindered their every step.

"I can't believe that we are on the right path. Peggy couldn't have easily marched Carrie through this mess. We are having to cut our way through. We have to go back and find a clearer path," said Randy.

As they traipsed back through the brush, Randy wondered if Melinda could provide any reference to help find Carrie.

"Sheriff, can we speak to Melinda? Maybe she could give us a clue to where Carrie is," said Randy

"They took her to a hospital in Okmulgee. She was found close to there. It's quite a ways from here, though. I can get in touch with the sheriff there and have him ask her some questions."

The sheriff of Okmulgee County was still at the hospital and was allowed in to see Melinda for a short period of time. In spite of all that she had been through, her injuries were slight. She was greatly dehydrated and had infections where her blisters were. That could have proved to be serious if they had not caught them in time. She also had a light concussion from her head hitting the rocks.

"Melinda, I am the sheriff in this area. Could I ask you some questions?"

Melinda raised heavy eyelids and nodded.

"There are several law enforcement individuals at the house where we believe a lady named Peggy had you captive. They are searching for a missing OSBI agent. There were two sets of tracks leading from the house into the woods, but they can't find where Peggy might have taken the agent. Can you think of anything that might help them find her?"

Melinda laid for a moment and then her eyes grew wide and she replied, "The box. She must have put her in the box."

~

When hearing Melinda's response over the phone, Randy wasn't sure the girl was fully lucid. But with further questioning, Melinda described in detail about the box and how Peggy had supposedly rescued her.

She didn't know exactly where the box was or how far from the house it was, but knew it was in a small clearing over an hour's walk from the house.

When she had told them everything she could for the moment, Randy ended the call and in seconds had Bracket sending a helicopter to them. They would search by air. Surely they would find the clearing and the box that way.

Randy's mind raced. Could Carrie survive a severe concussion and blood loss trapped in a metal box? And what about the rain? The deluge earlier had been a torrential downpour releasing several inches of rain at once. Could it have flooded the box?

The helicopter was at least thirty minutes out. Randy grabbed the map and searched for any sign of a clearing in the area, but none revealed itself to him. The map was zoomed out so that the woods consumed any small clearings and rendered them invisible.

Frustrated, Randy went back to the place he had lost the trail. Standing there, he tried to calm himself in order to think clearly. He looked at the surrounding areas. There was no actual sign of a path that Peggy could have taken. The earlier search had trampled much of the area, so there would be no sign left by Peggy and Carrie.

Randy continued to stand and look at each leaf and twig, searching for something, anything.

After a few minutes of combing the area, Randy spotted a drop of blood on a leaf. He had missed it several times before, but the lowering sun was now glinting just right to reveal it. From there, he followed one droplet after another for the next hour, straight to a small clearing.

In the box, Carrie was drifting away with no desire to return. Her head ached beyond any pain she could imagine. The water sloshed around her head and did nothing to comfort her. The desire to stretch out her legs was moot. There was no room in the box at all.

She was a fighter, but the fight had left her hours ago, so she slept half comatose.

There in the middle of the clearing, Randy saw the small metal box sunk level with the ground. A small divot on one side made room for a latch to cover a protruding loop for a padlock. Fortunately, there was no padlock, but the latch hung tightly to the loop preventing the lid from being opened.

He quickly released the latch and threw back the lid. There inside was Carrie.

Sunlight blazed into the box as the lid was thrust open and Randy stood silhouetted, but Carrie wouldn't have known. She was unconscious and unaware of her rescue.

At first, Randy couldn't tell if she was alive or not. The rain had only filled the box with about two inches of water, but she looked horrible. The side of her face was black and blue.

Blood crusted the side of her face and matted her hair. She was holding her hands together where her blood-soaked shirt had attempted to stop the flow of blood from the deep cut on her hand.

She didn't respond to their attempts to rouse her, but two fingers on her neck found a pulse. Randy reached in and scooped up his partner. She lay limp in his arms. He then relinquished her over to the helicopter rescue team who had landed just after he had found the box, and waved goodbye.

Epilog

Randy stood by Carrie's hospital bed as she opened her eyes. Neither spoke for what seemed like a lifetime, but the looks they exchanged spoke volumes.

They had taken Carrie to a hospital in Tulsa, the nearest large city, where she spent a week recovering. She had a hematoma where Peggy had hit her in the head with the shovel. Her hand was stitched and her blood supply restored.

In a hoarse raspy voice, Carrie asked, "Did you find Melinda?"

"We did. She had quite the story to tell. It seems Peggy had a wave of guilt and let her go, but then she wandered forever in the woods, going mostly in circles. Then, she wound up floating down the river on a makeshift raft, where she nearly drowned before two boys saw her.

"We also found Peggy. After she put you in the box, she took off in your car. Since we had an APB out on your car, she was pulled over by the highway patrol on the Turner Turnpike going towards Tulsa and arrested. She became distraught and gave up the entire story."

"Emily?" Carrie asked.

"We even found Emily. She wound up in Arkansas. She had some severe injuries and was in a coma for a couple of days. But she is awake now and will be fine. Her ankle had been badly broken and cut and was left virtually untended. The doctors nearly had to amputate, but they got to it in time and were able to save it. It will be a long recovery for her, but she is young and will, in time, recover completely.

"The lady who had bought Emily shot herself, which left Emily incapacitated on the sofa in the living room. She couldn't move and there was no sign of a phone. She heard an engine and struggled to crawl to the door. Then blacked out on the front porch. But a man looking for his dog found her and took her to the hospital.

"Both women were unmarried and childless and thought they could buy a child to love. They were told that the 'service' would put the girls in the box and that when the women pretended to find and in essence rescue them, the girls would be so thankful that they would love them.

"But they found you can't buy love or force it. It must be freely given, or it isn't love at all."

Carrie lay thinking about what Randy was saying. All of this from a dire need to be loved. How desperate they must have been to believe they could buy a child to love them.

"Did you find who was behind all of this?" Carrie asked.

Randy shook his head. "No. We tracked the phone numbers from the messages left at Peggy's house, but they were clever. They used random remote pay phones around the state."

"Where did the women find this child-buying service, anyway?"

"Peggy said that she saw a small line ad in the back of a local newspaper. It read something like 'adopt an orphan who needs a loving home.' Apparently, the payment took all of Peggy's life savings. She mailed them cash to a rented box at a store that rents postal boxes, and they mailed her instructions back to find the box with Melinda in it. We are trying to find more out, but the P.O. box was rented with cash and the name they used was bogus."

A tap on the door revealed Sherri Valencia. "Am I interrupting?"

"Not at all. I think I have just about filled Carrie in on everything. I'll go get some coffee and let you two visit."

Randy left, and Sherri walked into the room, pulling a chair close to Carrie's bedside. She sat thoughtfully, looking at Carrie for a moment before softly saying, "I know you don't believe in prayer, but I offer more than that, Carrie. If you ever just want to talk, I am a good listener."

Carrie nodded and searched Sherri's face. "You told me Melinda would be okay. You were certain of it. How did you know?"

Sherri sat for a moment, formulating the best response for someone who didn't believe in the supernatural. "You might call it gut instinct, but for me I knew. I received a divine understanding that God was watching over her and would deliver her back to us somehow, someway."

Carrie appreciated that Sherri was not pounding her with religion and just merely trying to explain how it was to her. Something about Sherri's confidence, and calmness in that confidence, drew Carrie to want to know more, but she just couldn't stomach the thought of religion.

"You were right. Melinda was okay. Sometimes, though, my gut instinct isn't right. Sometimes I don't know how to read my own instinct. Randy says I'm too impulsive and reckless."

"That is the difference in relying on our own understanding and relying on divine understanding. This isn't about religion, Carrie. It is about being connected to our divine creator in a real and personal way. A one-on-one intimate relationship."

Carrie shut her eyes. "Isn't that what religion is?"

"No. But many have twisted it into that. Through the centuries, man has tried to manipulate what was meant to be a precious relationship into a forced set of rules. That can't be done. It is a sad thing, but true.

"It is kind of like those women who thought they could buy someone to love. Many people think that if they create a strict set of rules and live by them, then it will buy God's love and acceptance. But that is all a lie. That is religion. You can't, and don't need to buy God's love. He freely and lovingly gives it."

Carrie laid there with her eyes still closed. What Sherri was saying to her was so far out in left field, she had no way of taking it in. And she still felt so battered and bruised that she didn't want to expend any precious mental energy thinking about it.

Just then, Randy came back in with coffee only for both he and Sherri. "I would have brought you a cup, but I wasn't sure you felt like coffee," said Randy

Carrie just shook her head. "I'm not up for coffee just now."

Sherri took the coffee from Randy, stood, and reached over to Carrie. "Give me a call sometime if you ever want to just talk. I am always here for you."

Carrie opened her eyes and saw what she believed to be genuine love and concern radiating from Sherri's eyes. It captured her, and she suddenly felt differently about their chaplain. "I will," said Carrie, and she meant it.

Authors Note

This novella is set two years after the prequel, Carrie Border, but seven years before the Redemption Series. I knew there was so much more to Carrie's story that needed to be told and that my readers would want to hear.

During the years between the prequel, and The Redemption Series, Carrie was working hard as an OSBI agent, and learning along the way. Not only were her skills improving, but so was her confidence, which sometimes led her to do dangerous and crazy things.

I thought I would fill that long gap with small novellas that focus more on the cases than her personal life while still giving us a barometer of how her personal life is going.

I do have plans for more full novels that will succeed The Redemption Series, while also providing more novellas in this same time period. Of course, there is the prequel that is scheduled for summer of 2024. You won't want to miss how Carrie's story with the OSBI began.

The places in this story such as Warr Acres, Welty, Okmulgee, and Okeema are true places. As are the stats on those counties.

There is a Wolfe Creek and a river named Deep Fork that winds like a red snake through central eastern Oklahoma.

As always, let me say that I have no true knowledge of how the OSBI or any other law enforcement agency works. I hold all law enforcement in high regard and in no way intend any disrespect with my inaccuracies. If they should happen to read them, I only hope they can laugh at my comical attempts to portray their immensely important jobs.

Remember, this is a work of fiction and I take great creative license in writing my novels. Nothing in this book should be used as fact. If there are mistakes, they are mine alone in spite of repeated edits.

Thank you for reading this book and I hope that you enjoy my other works. If you would, please leave a review on your favorite book review site.

About the Author

Nancy's love of writing fiction began in the seventh grade in literature class.

Through the years she has written magazine articles, newspaper articles, countless blog posts, and both fiction and nonfiction books. Many of those books have made it to the Amazon best seller ranking as well.

Nancy resides in Oklahoma in the state she was born. Always a creative person, she has done more types of arts and crafts than you can imagine. Recently, she has found a love for watercolor painting in her spare time.

In recent years, she has been a professional silversmith and also did studio jewelry training for silversmithing. She was also a licensed Oklahoma state Realtor but is now spending the bulk of her time writing.

Nancy feels that writing fiction for the sheer sake of entertainment is not good enough. She has always desired for her novels to touch her readers' lives and to even change them for the better in some small way. The many emails, texts, messages, and reviews she has received is a testament to that.

Other Works by Nancy Jackson

Novels

The Redemption Series

The Blood - Book 1

The Water - Book 2

The Fire - Book 3

The Redemption Series Box Set

The Box, a Carrie Border Novella

Carrie Border, The Prequel - coming soon (summer 2024)

Choices Like Rivers

Business Enrichment

How to Go From Hobby to Business

How to Write Publish and Market Your Book

Social Media Marketing Blitz Workbook and Planner

Please review this book and any others that you have read. It will help me more than you know!

www.ingramcontent.com/pod-product-compliance
Lightning Source LLC
Chambersburg PA
CBHW061216210726
48294CB00006B/1866
* 9 7 8 1 7 3 4 8 9 4 6 7 7 *